MORE ENDURING
FOR HAVING BEEN
BROKEN

www.blacklawrence.com

Executive Editor: Diane Goettel

Book and Cover Design: Zoe Norvell

Cover Art: "Pink Eucalyptus" by Leonie Cheetham

Copyright © Gwendolyn Paradice 2021

ISBN: 978-1-62557-832-7

Published 2021 by Black Lawrence Press.

Printed in the United States.

MORE ENDURING FOR HAVING BEEN BROKEN

AND OTHER SHORT STORIES

Gwendolyn Paradice

Black Lawrence Press

"An ending that confounds more than it concludes…
our reaction is to grip it closer.
To make our own connections and conclusions
where there is no material provided.
Our impetus is to find the satisfactory ending that has eluded us,
to walk away with an answer."

—CHRIS JAYNES, FROM MAT JOHNSON'S *PYM*

TABLE OF CONTENTS

AMARNA

I live in a god's city, but apparently, it's the wrong god. Mother says it's blasphemy to be here, and that god lives in churches, but father says god lives wherever he damn well pleases and if mother hasn't actually met him, maybe his vacation home just happens to be the place we take care of. This place is Amarna, and it's falling apart. Down, rather. I guess *apart* makes it sound like it's coming undone.

But it's okay that Amarna looks weathered, because it was built to look old. I tell the tourists that the city has stood for 3,346 years, but really, it's only been eleven. Father completed it the year I was born, and when I tell the tourists that the city is on the bank of the Nile river, I have to ignore the BillyBurger sign that's eight feet taller than our wall and whisper to them that this year the advisor has predicted the river will rise higher than normal and there's a chance the city might flood. The tourists drink out of plastic water bottles and smile politely. They feel sorry for the boy who's also a tour guide and they know, just as much as I do, that the only river Amarna is near is I-37 and that the bellows of the hippos I point out are actually honking car horns. I don't blame them for not believing. God appears only at sunrise, and we don't even open until ten.

*

You could say I work here, but I prefer the term "volunteer". There are pictures of me on the living room wall and I'm a year older in each of them, dressed in a white linen shendyt and smiling next to the sign that

1

reads, *Live the Past! Experience the home of Egypt's most infamous pharaoh, the heretic Akhenaton, here at AMARNA.* I only go into the details about how he wasn't *really* a heretic if someone is learned enough to know the history. There's one every few days or so, and they think they're really smart and bring it up like I don't know, but I shoot them down like an Ethiopian archer and say, in a voice that's too grown up for my skinny legs and lack of body hair, *People are often confused about the concept of advertising*, and then they ask how old I am.

I tell them I am eleven and a sophomore in high school and at first, they think I am lying. But then when I explain that I am homeschooled they either nod, like it's a sad thing, or open their eyes wider, assuming I'm too smart for public school, silently comparing me to their kids who complain about homework and demand cars when they turn sixteen. You know what I do for homework? Last week I made a pipe bomb that my mom actually helped me disassemble, and then I wrote a short story about a mathematics professor who came to think of real analysis as a type of philosophy. Sometimes I daydream about being a regular kid with a normal life, putting wires into potatoes and making light bulbs glow, or getting dropped off at the movie theatre then giving my parents angry looks when they don't drive off fast enough. But really, I like my life, and I love my parents. I tell them almost everything, but not how God comes to me in the morning and tells me his secrets.

*

I get up at 5:30 and fulfill my physical education requirement with my morning run. The circumference of Amarna is two miles, and when I'm done, I climb up the ramp into the ruins of the Small Aten Temple, flanked by columns made of mesh and fiberglass, constructed to look like stone, and I sit cross-legged facing East, waiting for Aten to appear.

He rises over the complex wall, sometimes weak and diluted by clouds, sometimes strong and hot and violent. He speaks to me as the last of his body clears the horizon, and every morning it's a small piece of knowledge, a koan for me to consider during the day. Sometimes I can't figure it out at all, but sometimes I come up with an answer. My favorite days are the ones in which I come up with an answer, but it *changes*. Those days, I really think I'm learning something.

This morning I am thankful for the breeze because it's already in the eighties and as the sun comes up I hear his voice like water rushing out of the tap, and though it's fierce and quick, it pools in my mind where it becomes clear and still and I wait until the water is tired and its surface is at rest and it whispers again and again until I commit the koan to memory. Today I hear, *when you can do nothing, what can you do?*

Like most days, I cannot comprehend what this could mean when I first hear it, but I repeat the question and whisper it to the breeze, and when I am sure I won't forget it, I walk back to our home in the King's House, where inside, instead of stone walls and dim, cloudy light, there is drywall and stiff Berber carpet and air fresheners called "Ocean Breeze" in white outlets against sage walls that make our home smell too strongly of coconut.

My mother is making breakfast and my father is on the phone with who I assume is Willa, the woman who runs the concession stand in what's left of the coronation hall where we sell lunches with prices the tourists complain about. But they can't resist the "Marinated Roasted Crocodile" (chicken), "Clay-Baked Hippo" (pork), and the popular "Amarna Dog," which is the cheapest thing on the menu and is clearly just a hot dog.

Father is sitting with his elbows on the kitchen table and one hand has the phone to his ear and the other is pressed over his eyes. *I know,* he says, *but maybe this isn't going to work.*

I know Willa is strange. She's in her forties and her hair is pink, a color that father has told her isn't authentic for the time, but Willa won't dye it a natural color and I wonder if father is finally going to let her go. Willa is what father calls an "independent contractor" and at night he stays up late and marks spreadsheets in red pen and he always has the checkbook out but never writes any checks.

Father looks up and sees me and is saying *yeah, yeah, yeah,* and then he hangs up and without a word leaves the room.

I sit across from where he was, and mother puts a plate in front of me: bagel and cream cheese and canned salmon and scrambled eggs. Next to this, she places a book.

What's this for? I ask her, fingering the crushed velvet cover with a name plate sewn onto the front. It's the book I see her reading every night in her bathrobe.

It's a bible, she says, stating the obvious.

I fork eggs onto my bagel. I don't like to eat food separately. *But what's it for?*

I think it's time we start doing things the right way around here. She's fingering the lace edge of her apron and trying to gauge my reaction.

Did you know that Christ is a representation of Horus? I ask her. *He's basically the same thing. I think the Christians copied the Egyptians.*

She frowns hard at me.

Solar deities are popular in many religions—

This place is poison, she says, and I'm surprised by how angry she sounds. I know mother would rather be in a regular house in the suburbs with a lawn to water and flowers to plant; father won't let her have a garden here. He says it wouldn't be authentic. But she never tells *me* how much she doesn't like it. She doesn't say it now, either. She says, *Your new class is Religious Studies and we're starting with Christianity.*

I am already doubtful that this class will study anything other than Christianity, but this week we're going to make a solar panel in science and so I'm willing not to argue about this one thing. *When you can do nothing, what can you do?* I think about the question and decide that when I can do nothing, I will accept it and not complain. It seems like the right answer. An adult answer.

But it also annoys me.

It's too easy.

While I eat, mother bangs the pan loudly in the sink and the front door closes. I open the bible blindly and read Proverbs 29:25: *The fear of man bringeth a snare, but whoso putteth trust in the Lord shall be safe.*

I don't want to make my mother angry by telling her that I don't believe in her god. Maybe learning more about Christianity might be a good thing. Any knowledge is productive.

I close the bible and see that I've left a white cream-cheese fingerprint on the aged velvet. I quickly rub it off, but it leaves a milky smear. *We're out of toothpaste*, I remind her, and she becomes very still.

Her back is to me and she says, *Today's history lesson is how the ancients used to make toothpaste.*

Will it work? I ask, rubbing my tongue over fuzzy teeth.

I don't know yet.

*

You can see by these reliefs that the Egyptian canon of art was modified during Akhenaton's reign. I am showing a group of tourists the elongated bodies of the royal family with their hands outstretched towards the solar disk.

They were aliens, a man says.

I turn towards him, still smiling. *It's true that the representations of the human form are altered*, I explain, *but many experts believe that this was intentional and that Akhenaton wanted to distinguish his new way of life from the old by offering alternative depictions.*

Aliens built the pyramids too, he says, as if he's an Egyptologist and studied in Cairo.

I know his type. He is scared of foreign ideas and he's wearing a black shirt with a bald eagle clutching an American flag in its talons and his fanny pack is unzipped to reveal a crushed box of Marlboros.

I'm not saying it was aliens, a woman next to him declares, *but it was aliens.* She is smiling to herself and trying not to laugh and I smile wider at her. She's making fun of him, and he doesn't understand exactly how she's doing it, but he knows he's being challenged and frowns at her.

When you can do nothing, what can you do? Keep smiling and let the stupid be stupid, I think.

We have a wonderful book on Amarna period art, I say to the crowd, eleven people: two families and two single adults. *Our souvenir shop has great resources if you're interested in continuing your learning experience at home.*

The eagle-shirt-wearing-man's daughter has her arms crossed and I know they won't be buying any books.

With that, I pronounce, *our tour is concluded. Please visit our snack stand and enjoy the authentic taste of ancient Egyptian cuisine.*

The group doesn't ask any questions, and they leave the temple through the front doors. Only one woman remains behind.

Do you *have any questions?* I ask her.

Not really, she says. She is older, with dark blonde hair put up in a bun, and she doesn't look like a normal tourist. She is wearing a navy skirt suit and her pink lipstick clashes. We stand there, and I am waiting for her to leave so I can go get lunch too. It's noon and I'm hungry.

How old are you? she asks.

Eleven.

And you work here?

My parents own Amarna.

Don't you go to school?

I'm home schooled, I explain.

She nods. *Don't you ever want to go to a regular school? Hang out with kids your own age?*

Not really.

So you don't mind wearing that, she asks, nodding to my costume.

No. I'm told girls like a guy with a tan anyway, I joke.

She laughs and opens her purse. She pulls out her wallet.

Please, ma'am, no tips. If you'd like you can make a donation in the souvenir store.

She takes two steps forward and instead of handing me money she hands me a business card. *My name is Lisa Halpin. I've been assigned as your new case worker.*

I don't understand for a minute, and then I realize what is going on. *You're with CPS?* I ask, taking the card and looking down at it. Her name is printed in boring black font and there's a phone number too. *I don't need a case worker,* I tell her.

I know you don't need *one*, she assures me, *but if you ever want to talk…*

If you know I don't need one, then there's no reason for you to be here. I am eleven *but I am* not *stupid.*

We're concerned about you, she says, as if the whole world has been watching me and is collectively anxious for my well-being.

You should maybe talk to my parents, I say warily. I don't like being confronted this way and I feel like she's being sneaky.

Yes, maybe I should. Can you tell me where I can find the office?

I tell her where my father is, and she smiles. *You can call me any time.*

Okay, I say, but I know I won't.

*

Outside, there are a few people milling about. I decide I don't want to eat at home and go to the snack stand to get an Amarna dog from Willa. The man who believes in aliens is there with his wife and daughter and they're sitting on stone benches under one of the white canopies in the courtyard.

Hi Willa, I say, and she opens the metal cart with the steaming water. She knows what I like, and there's already a bun in her hand.

Hey Jacob, she says. I like the way she says my name. I don't know where she's from, but she pronounces the second syllable like "cob," and I appreciate that because it is a short O, not a U. *You talked to your dad today?* She puts the hot dog in the bun and then puts the whole thing in an oblong plastic basket.

No, I tell her, and pump three squirts from the ketchup into a paper cup.

Oh. She seems disappointed.

He should be in his office, but I think he's talking to someone right now. I don't tell Willa about the CPS woman. She looks like she wants to say something more, but doesn't.

Not many people here today, I offer. The hot dog is wet and my bun is a little soggy.

Not many people lately, she complains, and she's right. Seems like the last couple of years fewer and fewer people have been coming. I *think I'm going to have to get a different job.*

But you can't leave, I tell her. *What are the people going to eat?*

She points over the wall at the BillyBurger sign. *Listen, Jacob. I'm going to leave*, she admits. *I bought a food truck and already paid rent for a spot over at the university. I wanted to tell you myself. I'm just not making it here.*

Does my father know?

I'm going to tell him today, she says. *But please let me do it, okay? I owe him that much.*

Yeah. Okay. You're still going to come by, though, right? And visit?

She doesn't respond right away, and I know she won't.

Hey Jacob, do you ever think it might be good to, you know, be in school? There aren't a lot of people for you to talk to here.

I look at her, and I can tell by the way she's not really looking at me, but looking at the American alien family, that she might be the one who's been calling CPS. I put the half-eaten hot dog on the cart between us. *Thanks for lunch, Willa. Maybe I'll see you sometime.*

Wait, Jacob.

But I'm already walking away.

*

From one to four I do schoolwork. Today my mother has left a list of my lesson plans and a note that she's gone to do errands. I am supposed to read about gene mutation and 3D geometry, and then I'm supposed to work on my Shakespeare paper. We're reading *Hamlet*, but I don't know why because *Hamlet* is so over-studied. I decide I don't want to write about *Hamlet* at all and instead of doing science and math I start to read *As You Like It*. Shakespeare's comedies were always my favorite.

When I am done with reading, I do an activity where I tape an equilateral triangle over our globe and learn that the angles are all 90 degrees. The gene mutation chapter is kind of boring, and I don't have any interest in bean pods. I read ahead and see that next week I'll learn about fruit flies and that I'll get to put them in the freezer, stun them, and look at them under the microscope.

At five, I am supposed to walk the complex, check the buildings to make sure there aren't any stragglers, and then lock the gate. I keep my costume on while I do this. I don't want to ruin the authenticity of Amarna.

The food cart area is closed up, and I see that Willa has taken her Amarna dog cart and the chip display rack. I swing by the front office and my father is inside on the phone. He's arguing with someone and so I grab the keys, wave at him, and make my rounds. At the end, I stop at the Small Aten Temple and think about my koan.

When you can do nothing, what can you do?

I don't know what the answer is. Some days it's like this. I can come up with *an* answer, but don't feel like it's *the* answer. I decide that maybe there isn't an answer, that the koan is circular and that maybe the answer is something like, when you can do nothing, you think about what you can't do, like answer a koan.

When I get back to the king's palace at six there is no dinner, but my mother is in the kitchen, and she is sitting at the table with a suitcase on the floor beside her.

What's going on? I ask her.

We're going to grandpa's house, she says.

Why?

She looks uncomfortable and shuffles her feet under the table. *Because it's not working here.*

What's not working? I get a feeling in my stomach, like a hot walnut is in my gut, and I refuse to step any farther into the room. My mother looks old and worn and for the first time I really see how tired she must be, because she's not wearing any makeup and there are dark circles under her eyes.

This. This, she says, gesturing to the room. *Everything.*

It's great, I protest.

No, it's not. She says this the way the man in the eagle shirt said that aliens built the pyramids. *Go change your clothes. We can talk about this in the car.*

No! I say, and I realize she's gotten louder and I'm getting louder too. *I'm not leaving!*

We are *leaving*, she says, and she stands up. *Go change your clothes.*

I'm not going! I yell.

Stop being a child.

I'm not *a child! I work and I go to school and I teach myself stuff and I'm smarter than you.*

I said it. I said what I've been thinking for the past year and I can tell by the way her face is pale that she knows it's true.

You know what? she asks, and she says it quietly. *You're not a child. And that's my fault. You talk to your dad tonight. If you're not a child you're old enough to know what's really going on. When you talk to him, you call me at grandpa's, and I'll come get you.*

Is this about the CPS lady? I ask, and I'm almost crying now because I don't want my mother to leave, and I've just said something mean, but I'm not going to take it back because I know it's the truth, and I don't want to leave Amarna.

Partly. She picks up the suitcase. It's grey and purple flannel and I remember that the last time I saw it was when we went to Washington to see the museum complex. *Talk to your dad.*

She is walking out and I yell at her, *We don't have any toothpaste!*

We don't have any money for toothpaste, she says.

*

Hours later, father doesn't come home, and when I go to the office he is at his desk and papers are everywhere. I don't want to talk to him, yet, I decide.

I go to the closet where we keep our camping gear and pull out my sleeping bag. I get the pillow off my bed and don't feel like changing into my pajamas.

On the way to the Small Aten Temple it is quiet and dark and the stars are dim. Last week, I learned about different types of stars and even though I knew already that our sun is a star, I was kind of angry that it was lumped in with all the others. It's a special star. And not just because it's the closest one to our planet. It's special because God lives there, and I know he does because he talks to me and gives me mysteries to unravel and it's unfair that other people will never be able to know this.

All other stars besides the sun are puny. Twinkle is a stupid word and these stars do that stupid thing. They don't blaze and heat like the sun. Maybe somewhere in outer space they're boiling and exploding, but I can't tell that. I've *seen* pictures of the sun, solar flare magma arcing across the surface, and that is real and powerful.

I unroll my sleeping bag in the ruins and look up at the sky. I wait for the sun to come up.

*

I don't remember falling asleep but when I wake up, I am stiff and my right shoulder hurts from where I've been laying on it. My shendyt is rolled up around my waist and no one's around to see me in my underwear, but for some reason, I'm embarrassed anyway. My father has clearly been here. There's a water bottle and some cookies on the stone altar next to me. I don't know if they're for me or Aten.

I sit cross-legged on my sleeping bag as the sky lightens. I don't know if I should call my mother or not. I don't know if I should talk to my father. I know I'll have to do both, but I am waiting for Aten to speak to me first.

When the sun breaches the horizon, I wait for the water words, but none come. The only thing I hear is my own voice asking, *when you can do nothing, what can you do*, and I think the answer is *wait*.

ADELINE'S FARM FOR EXPLODING CHICKENS

The sign about five miles down county road FM 423 is easy to miss. The post oaks are tall and ungroomed, the scraggly branches fighting for sunlight, splaying their many-fingered limbs so that the hand-carved wooden proclamation is almost completely obscured. My grandma made the sign, her old-fashioned pyrography worn and faded now. On a bad day it can't be seen at all. On a good day, one made of sunlight and breezes, the branches get hooked behind the wooden rectangle and are held back so the name of this place is visible: *Adeline's Farm for Exploding Chickens*.

Once or twice a year there's an eager-joke tourist crawling up the gravel drive in their car, the crunch enough to send me running—*don't slam the door!*—down the drive, waving hands, mouthing *stop stop*. Gotta explain to them that the chickens are sensitive, easily scared, and yes, they may see them, but they must turn off their cars right away. Why grandpa doesn't put in a gate is beyond me. Secretly, I think he might like the attention. But the visitors would never be able to tell, his right eye drooping with edema, his teeth bared yellow through grimaces shaded by years of tobacco.

He used to be famous. For a year or so. When ma was an actress, she told her producers about her family and then they'd made commercials about *Adeline's Farm for Exploding Chickens*, starring ma, of course, standing beside *her* ma, both of them hawking eggs. That was back in the day when TVs had convex screens, when rabbit ears were coated in tin foil. In greyscale, I could still make out the differences of grandma's skin, her right arm a map of pink scar tissue and freckles. Maybe other people noticed too, and because of this no one wanted the eggs, a hint of danger at breakfast. Of course, like any old egg, the ones we sell aren't fertilized. No cake is going to explode. No eggs benedict will burst into flames at the table. The chickens only blow up if they're startled.

*

Crockett is leaning her head against the car window. It's hot and though it feels like her scalp might be reddening, she doesn't move. *Penance* is a word she knows with her body, the way she knows Andy Johnson with her body now too. She puts down the book, keeping one finger on the page she hasn't finished reading.

In the driver's seat, her older sister is on the phone with their mother who is away in Las Vegas getting married for the fourth time. Greg Monce is a cattle man she met at the Rusty Nail and Crockett does not like him—the way he barges into every conversation and tries to make the topic applicable to himself; the way when he sleeps at their house and he only stays in their mother's room half the time, the other half up late on the sofa drinking Jim Beam so that every time Crockett needs to use the toilet she has to walk through the room; the way when she does this Greg Monce watches her, his hand on the bottle between his legs, his face swallowed by TV light; the way she's said all this to her mother who shrugs it off with the lamest reasons for his behavior and then says, "he's got money comin' you know."

Crockett's sister doesn't have to deal with this crap. She's got a full scholarship to Texas A&M where she studies agriculture and has a job waiting tables at a chain restaurant. She hasn't been home in over three months and is only here now because their mother has run off for two weeks and Crockett doesn't know how to drive. Someone has to get groceries. Someone has to go pay the bills—always with cash because they don't have internet access and because there's not enough money to pay bills in advance. Someone has to pick up Crockett from the police station after she's found passed out and full of booze at the community pool next to the half-naked Andy Johnson. Thankfully the cherry Slurpee she'd mixed with vodka had, at some point, been knocked into the pool, cleansed by chorine, so Crockett had escaped a minor in possession charge. After almost five hours in the drunk tank—a concrete cinder-block room smelling like urine and puke with a metal toilet that wouldn't flush properly—her sister came to take her back home.

Crockett's sister is listening to their mother but the hand she's using to steer is making "talk-talk" signs and she's rolling her eyes. "They're not pressing charges or anything," she says in Crockett's defense. "No. No. Just relax. I got it under control." Then loudly she says to Crockett, "Mom wants you to know that she's really angry at you. And disappointed."

Crockett's head is aching and her eyes hurt. She knows something about disappointment too.

"Mom says that when she gets back you need to start going to church. She says you're out of control and that someone needs to put the fear of God in you."

Crockett decides to stop listening.

When her sister hangs up, Crockett asks about the book. So far high school has been full of stuff she doesn't like reading: *Huckleberry Finn*, *The Red Badge of Courage*, *To Kill a Mockingbird*. Crockett isn't a big reader to begin with, having given up reading when she was ten and her mother threw out the *Zoo Book* collection she'd managed to amass—*crud*, her mother had called them. *Crud junking up the house.* Crockett never quite recovered from that betrayal.

"Where did you find this? What's an exploding chicken farm?" The book Crockett is talking about is slim and oddly shaped: too tall and too narrow. Numbers only appear on the left-hand sides of pages and the pages themselves are thick and crisp, not thin and brittle like the books the school gives them. It's titled *An Unfortunate History of Adeline's Farm for Exploding Chickens,* but there is no author, no publisher that Crockett can find.

Her sister laughs. "That? Someone left it at a Whataburger off I-35. Weird huh? I only got through page 8 before I had to leave."

"You just took it?" Crockett is surprised at this. Her sister is the golden child, the one who gets good grades, ignores boys, and doesn't steal.

"I'm *borrowing* it. I'll drop it off on my way back."

Crockett wishes her sister wouldn't go back. She wishes her sister would stay in this awful podunk town and get a job at IHOP or Walmart. Then when Crockett graduates, they can get a place together. Crockett has already decided college isn't for her.

She looks at the cover. There is a small boy in the foreground, but she can't see his face. His head is turned around, looking back at a farmhouse that is exploding. There are chickens everywhere.

"Do exploding chickens exist?" Crockett asks.

Her sister laugh-snorts. "That's some good schooling you're getting if you're asking that."

Crocket frowns.

Her sister seems to know what she's said cuts to the core, so she amends, "Not that I know of. Probably not. Feel like we would have known if there were. That's all fiction, Crockett, made up."

Crockett remembers this word from her English class, but she's always confused fiction and non-fiction, can never remember which was true and which wasn't.

"Besides, sounds like it would be a disaster, doesn't it? I mean, look at the cover."

Crockett looks again, but this time she notices something else. The boy is fleeing the farmhouse through the property's gate which reads, *Adeline's Farm for Exploding Chickens, Krum, Texas.*

"Did you see this? It says Krum."

Crockett's sister tries to look but says, "I can't read and drive at the same time. Probably some local wrote it. Self-published. Anyone can write anything these days."

Crockett wonders when her sister started knowing things like this, about self-publishing and macro-nutrients in food and how Pluto isn't a planet anymore.

The car pulls into the drive of their small three-bedroom home. Their mother has recently taken to decorating the brick exterior near the front door with metal crosses. Most are old and kind of rusted—*quaint* or *antique*, their mother says—but Crockett thinks it makes them look forgotten and un-cared for. If their mother is going to find a renewed interest in God, at least she can make it look like she's trying.

"Look, kid," Crockett's sister begins.

Crockett hates it when her sister calls her kid—they are only five years apart in age.

Crockett's sister has turned off the car and Crockett finally pulls her head away from the window. "I know all this is hard. I get it. I really do. But if you keep doing shit like this—mom told me about the locker thefts and failing your classes—you're never going to get out of here. You gotta suck it up for a while. Behave."

Crockett's sister does not understand what is going on at all, but Crockett's head aches and she does not want to argue right now. Right now she wants to go to sleep, to drink all the water in the world, to delete Andy Johnson's number from the caller ID because she is so embarrassed. This is all easy for her sister to say, anyway. She never fucked up like Crockett. She started at the top. Crockett was never there to begin with.

*

My ma is on the television. She looks different, prettier, younger.

"That it?" My grandma asks. "Johnny! It's on!"

My grandpa rushes in, blood still on his hands. From the kitchen I can smell hot grease. "Well, I'll be."

My ma is standing in a kitchen that's not ours. The kitchen she's in is big, and the floor is checkered. There's a nice table in it too, but it has no chairs. She's standing at it and in front of her is a carton of eggs, a mixing bowl, and a bag of flour. An announcer speaks over her. *Maybe you've used our competitors' eggs, but you should be using Adeline's Eggs.*

"That's me!" my grandma says, scooting to the edge of the sofa.

My ma picks up the carton. She eyes it skeptically, but she's smiling too. I don't know why she's so dolled up, her hair done, and in a dress you'd never find on a farm. Her lips are dark and her lashes are thick.

When you're raising a growing boy, you want the best for him. Adeline's eggs come from special chickens, raised by a good family, and brought straight to your local market.

Then my ma is replaced by a cartoon chicken. The chicken is smiling too. It's walking around the barn yard carrying eggs in its wings. It trips and one egg flies off screen.

Then it's my grandma, in the kitchen, across from my ma. Grandma looks different too. She's all dressed up and has a handkerchief in her hair. With the way she's turned I can barely see the scars on her arm, the right side of her face. She catches an egg and holds it up, inspecting it.

She nods and hands it to my ma, who cracks it into a bowl.

When you care about your family, you do what's best for them.

Then my grandma speaks, but it doesn't sound like her. It's halting and unnatural. "Adeline cares about your family too. That's why all our eggs are always inspected, to make sure only the best ones reach your table."

The bowl in front of my mother is gone. In its place is a chocolate cake. My grandma is gone too, and a boy rushes in, bouncing on the balls of his feet.

I wonder why if ma and grandma are in the commercial, I've been replaced with this unknown child.

Buy Adeline's eggs.

When the commercial is over my grandpa says, "You look as gorgeous as the day I met you." He leans over and kisses the back of my grandma's head.

She closes her eyes while he does.

"Are people going to want eggs from exploding chickens?" I ask. "When is ma coming home?"

*

"Hey," Crockett says. Her sister is sitting at the table in the kitchen. She is balanced in the chair, tipped back on two legs, and in her lap is a bowl of cereal. She's watching the small 12-inch TV that their mother always has on while cooking. "Do you think you could take me to the library?"

Her sister picks grain flakes from between her teeth. She doesn't respond for almost a minute. On the TV, Lucille Ball is applying wallpaper in her bedroom, but it is going horribly. Somehow, she's managed to get it all wrapped around herself. "*Really?* The *library?* You can tell me, you know."

"No for real I need to go to the library. I gotta check something out."

"Well look at you," Crockett's sister says, reaching to set the bowl on the table, the chair creaking, one of the spokes in the back popping out of place. "Damnit."

Crockett stands, waiting for an answer. Maybe her sister really doesn't believe her. Last time Crockett asked for a ride somewhere she'd had to call her sister at one in the morning from the next town over when her "friend" from a house party left without telling her. "There's this book that's mentioned, in the uh, chicken book."

"Chicken book?"

"Yeah, the book you stole from Whataburger?"

Crockett's sister is inspecting the chair leg, pops it back into its socket. "Borrowed. Yeah right I forgot about it. Are you reading that crappy thing? If you want something to read I can recommend stuff. In lit we read *Tess of the D'Urbervilles*. Thomas Hardy is such a badass. Such a nihilist."

Crockett doesn't know what *nihilist* means and doesn't ask. She's hurt that her sister is so quick to dismiss the chicken book; she kind of expected her sister to encourage the reading, to say something like, *Hey kid, that's awesome! I'm glad you like it. You can learn so much cool stuff from books.* "Never mind. I can call Andy," she says, already knowing what her sister's reaction will be.

"Nuh-uh. That guy is nothing but bad news. I'll take you. I need to check my email anyway. I don't know why mom just won't get the fucking internet already."

*

When Crockett walks into the library she realizes she doesn't know what to do. She's never even been in her high school's library.

This is the worst kind of maze. One without an end. Crockett has to get her sister's help at the card catalog, and when they don't find the book Crockett is looking for, she wanders the aisles for twenty minutes before giving up. There's chickens in the farming section, kids' books about chickens, the history of chickens. But nothing about exploding chickens.

The reference librarian at the front desk is a stereotype. Her grey hair is coiled at the nape of her neck and she wears reading glasses and a cardigan.

"Excuse me," Crockett says, clearing her throat. "Can you help me find something?"

The woman looks up.

"I'm looking for something called *Wonders of the East*."

The woman turns to her keyboard. Does some clacking.

Crockett's sister is across the room on one of the public access computers. She's smiling and twirling a piece of her hair.

"Do you know the author?" The woman is squinting at the screen even though she's wearing her glasses now.

"Um. No. But it's old. Really old."

"Let me just try WorldCat."

Crockett doesn't know what WorldCat is and she imagines some giant, rounded feline, floating in outer space, batting the moon with its paw.

"It's about exploding chickens," Crockett clarifies.

"Exploding? What?"

"Exploding chickens." Crockett feels stupid repeating it.

The woman presses keys. Clicks her mouse. "You sure *Wonders of the East* is what you want? Here's one, but it's a translation of an Old English manuscript."

Crockett isn't sure that this is what she wants, and so she says nothing.

"Why don't you use the computers," the woman suggests. "Do some research. If you want it, I can get it through library loan."

Crockett doesn't know what library loan is either, but she finds an open computer next to her sister and clicks on the internet. In the search bar she types with two fingers, *wonders of the east exploding chickens.*

The first thing that comes up is a link to something she can't pronounce, but the summary says *burning hens.*

"What's that?" her sister asks, leaning over to look at the screen. "An academic journal article?"

Maybe that's what it is. Crockett can't get through the language. It's too difficult.

"What are you looking for?"

"Exploding chickens." She's had to say it for the third time now. "The Whataburger book says exploding chickens came from some book called *Wonders of the East.*"

"You can search for that. Here." Crockett's sister presses keys on Crockett's board and types in *chickens.* She presses enter and a word on the page becomes highlighted in blue: *incendiary chickens.*

"What's incendiary?" Crockett asks.

"It means 'catches fire.'"

Crockett tells the woman at the desk that yes she wants the book. The librarian tells her that it will arrive within a week, probably, and asks Crockett if she has an account. Crockett has to make one, and the woman says she needs a phone number so they can call her when it comes in. Crockett isn't sure the landline will work in a week, so she gives the woman her sister's number.

Back at the computers, Crockett's sister is on Facebook. She is sending messages with someone Crockett doesn't know.

Crockett searches *Granbury to Krum distance.* It is 81 miles away.

*

The summer my grandma was exploded, we started trying to figure out a way to stop the chickens from causing too much damage. We tried metal henhouses, but the chickens wouldn't go inside. Too much like an oven in the Texas sun, and they weren't ready to be cooked yet.

We tried just letting them roam, but there was drought that summer too, and one of them popped in the old cow pasture and started a grass fire.

Finally, grandpa and I set up a wire fence around the burnt-up cow pasture and put them out there. Only one more popped that summer, and that was my fault. I was walking them back to the barn—can't leave them out at night for coyotes and wild dogs or the whole flock would explode—and Peter Pan wasn't having it.

I got everyone else inside, but Peter Pan made a run for the herb patch. I was chasing him, the way grandpa taught me to. Not too fast, thinking about how he might move, thinking about where I needed to move to corral him in the right direction.

I guessed wrong and Peter Pan scrambled away towards Bettie, our donkey. Bettie wasn't having it either and ee-haw'd and started running from the chicken and Peter Pan went bam!

That was the last donkey we had.

When ma came back after the funeral and moved into the barn, the chickens were never scared of her. She had a way with animals like she didn't have with people, and because the chickens didn't care that she had a kid out of wedlock and didn't care about her failed auditions, she didn't care about their pitfalls either.

I think that's why they worked—her and the chickens—because they both understood that only people will blame you when you make a mistake or fail.

At dusk I'd herd the chickens towards the barn, and ma would always be there with the door open, dressed in her finest, welcoming them home. They never ran from her the way they tried to run from me.

They ran *towards* her even, clucking and flapping their useless wings.

In the barn she'd spread chicken feed on the picnic table and sit with them while they pecked. She'd tell them how wonderful they were doing, congratulate them on how many eggs they produced. She'd give me her dinner tray and a basket of eggs, then send me off so she could practice her lines with them.

"Remember, this is going to be dangerous."

"…You don't know what danger means."

*

When the phone rings, Crockett is sure it's the library. And then she remembers she gave the library her sister's number, not the home phone, but it's too late. She's already picked up the call, and her mom's cell phone number glows on the screen.

"You just wouldn't believe," her mother says about Vegas. "You wouldn't believe how bright it is at night. You wouldn't believe the food. You wouldn't believe it's possible to sleep all day. You wouldn't believe the show. You wouldn't believe, believe, *believe.*"

Of course Crockett would believe. She *does* believe. She believes her mother is having the time of her life while Crockett sits at home and doesn't watch TV because the cable's been cut off.

"Greg is *just* the sweetest man."

Crockett has never known Greg Monce to be sweet. She can see him in his ironed jeans, fat hands at her mother's waist. Fat hands at a slot machine.

"You wouldn't believe how many kinds of slots there are."

Not just cherries and pots of gold and the number 7. A slot machine based on the movie *Aliens. Star Wars. Superman.* A slot machine for ancient Egypt. A slot machine that's a used car lot. A slot machine under the sea. A slot machine for the Wild West.

"You wouldn't believe... a slot machine based on the Bible. I won 100 dollars."

"Good. Then maybe when you get back you can turn the cable back on." Crockett is sitting on the kitchen counter. She thinks the thermostat she's looking at may be broken. It says the house is 75 but she knows it's hotter than that.

"Cable-schmayble," her mom says. "Besides, we ate at Wolfgang Puck's restaurant at Caesar's Palace. You wouldn't believe how much that cost."

Crockett's sister ambles in. "Why doesn't the TV work?"

Crockett passes the phone to her sister, sliding off the counter and opening the fridge. She hears her sister ask, "You married now?"

Through the front window, Crockett sees Andy Johnson's truck pull into the drive, and she goes to the front door.

"Aren't brides supposed to wear white?" her sister says into the phone.

Andy Johnson doesn't look as good when Crockett is sober. In the daylight she can see his calves are fat. As he steps onto the porch, she notices the baseball hat he's wearing is dark with sweat. She slowly locks the screen door.

He looks shaded through the mesh, standing just inside the shadow of the porch. He looks pixelated and as he moves on the other side, Crockett's eyes get dizzy.

"So," he says, shoving his hands into his pockets. "Why won't you answer my calls?"

"So," Crockett says back, unwilling to answer his question.

They stand like this on either side of the door, Andy Johnson wanting to say everything and Crockett wanting to say nothing.

"You get in trouble?" he finally asks, and Crockett shakes her head. "Good. I wouldn't want you to get in trouble."

"Mom's gone."

"Oh."

Inside, Crockett's sister is laughing.

"I thought…" Andy Johnson begins.

"I don't think we should see each other again," Crockett says. A fly is buzzing around Andy Johnson's head but he doesn't try to swat it away. What's the point? There's always another.

"Oh."

"I mean…" Crockett can't very well say she doesn't like him. She slept with him after all, and Andy Johnson isn't a bad guy, just not the kind of guy for Crockett. She can't just say she slept with him because she was curious, because he was there when she felt like it. "You know what the Bible says about…" she trails off. It's the only thing she can think of, and it makes her sick, almost, to say something like her mother might just to get out of an awkward conversation.

"Oh yeah, totally, I get it. But I mean, we don't have to do that again, if you don't want to."

Crockett wishes she had an exploding chicken. She'd toss it at Andy Johnson, and he'd catch it, or he wouldn't, but either way he'd explode and wouldn't be her problem anymore. Not a fair thought, she knows, but life isn't fair. If she worked on Adeline's farm she'd send chickens in the mail. She'd send a chicken to Greg Monce at the Rusty Nail. Hopefully it'd start a fire and burn down the whole damn bar with all her mom's ex-husbands inside. She'd send a chicken to Lizzy Meyer too, the girl who announced, to the entire class, that Crockett had left a red stain on her chair when Crockett had to wad up toilet paper and stick it in her underwear because she started her period for the first time in the middle of the day at school.

"We could just go for a drive," Andy Johnson suggests. "Go to the lake. Dairy Queen. I'd like to buy you an ice cream."

"Hey kid," Crockett's sister calls. "Mom wants you."

Crockett leaves Andy Johnson on the porch and takes the phone.

"We're comin' home," her mom says. "I need you to clean up a bit. Greg's selling his house."

"Yeah, whatever."

"For real Crockett, don't get an attitude." Her mom hangs up before Crockett can say anything more.

"He's selling the house." Crockett's sister thinks Crockett is saying this to her, but Crockett is saying it to herself. It doesn't really concern her sister who's going to go back to college, who doesn't have to live here with a man with stinky feet on her sofa.

"He's not selling it," Crockett's sister says. "He lost it."

"I'm going out with Andy Johnson."

"That him at the door?" Crockett's sister tries to be casual, but it's obvious she's looking because she has to come out of the kitchen, into the living room, in order to see him. "*He's* the one you got caught with?"

"Yeah."

"Well don't do anything stupid. You're smarter than that. You got what? Two more years? You can do two more years. I did."

*

Crockett orders a large vanilla cone and then asks the man behind the counter what kind of eggs they use.

"I dunno. Pre-mixed. Comes in a bag."

She and Andy Johnson sit outside even though it makes their ice cream melt faster. If Crockett had worried—even for a second—that Andy Johnson was going to want something in return for buying her a cone, she was wrong.

Instead of letting her know that she owes him one, he tells her that he likes to paint. He's not any good at real painting—people or animals or landscape—but he likes textures, so he mixes paint with dirt, paint with hair, collages flashy magazine covers and paints over them too. He shows her his hands, the paint under his fingernails, his stained fingertips. He says lava soap won't get it off. She suggests nail polish remover.

When they're done with ice cream, Andy Johnson buys them lunch too. *Reverse eating*, he calls it, grease dripping from his burger. When he sucks on his fingers, Crockett wonders if he's eating paint too.

"What do you do?" he asks her.

Crockett doesn't do much. She watches TV. She doesn't do her homework. She doesn't have the internet.

"But you have to be interested in something," Andy Johnson persists. "No one does nothing."

"I've been researching exploding chickens," she tells him.

"Well, that's new."

"Yeah, when they get scared they just blow up."

"Do they like, have a bomb in them? What makes them explode?"

"I'm not sure yet. I'm waiting on a book through library loan." She says this as if it's a common occurrence, ordering special books other people don't know about. For a minute, it makes her feel big. "I'm pretty sure they're born that way. It's not like some mad scientist shit."

"You interested in genetics? Science?"

Crockett has never given this much thought, but maybe yes, she is. Now that she thinks about it, she wants to know what makes the chickens work.

"It's kind of hard to believe," Andy Johnson says. His soda is empty and his straw slurps the bottom of the cup. "But I like the idea."

"There's a whole farm. Adeline's Farm for Exploding Chickens. It's in Krum. You know where that is?"

Andy Johnson shakes his head. "Crom? Like the god from *Conan the Barbarian*?"

"No. Maybe. It's not far, like an hour and a half away."

"Why don't you go there then?"

*

When Crockett returns home, her sister is gone, and there is a note on the kitchen table. *Library called. Your book is in. Gone to get mom and Greg. Plane's in at nine.*

Crockett takes the note outside and sets in on fire in the front yard with one of her new stepdad's lighters. Or does it belong to the one before him? Who knows. Her mom has a jar of lighters from men she's either married or slept with.

Crockett's supposed to clean up, but in the house there isn't a lot to do. She cleans the kitchen counter with a rag. She vacuums the living room. She's not sure what to do with the *stuff*. She is not going to do Greg's laundry. She is not going to dust her mother's Precious Moments cherub collection. She almost wishes it was not summer vacation. If she had homework, she'd do it.

Adeline's Farm for Exploding Chickens is on the table next to where the note used to be. If she knew how to drive she would go there. She'd take her mom's Taurus. She'd take what's left of the money her mom put on top of the fridge and go to the Quik Trip and buy a map. She'd buy pizza and sunflower seeds and Dr. Pepper.

That's the one good thing about not having a cell phone. No one can call to find out where you are when you take off.

If she could drive, she would at least go to the library and get that other book, the one about exploding chickens.

She wonders what it would be like to be an exploding chicken.

Do they know they can explode? Are they scared of their own explosiveness? Of others'? Are they committing suicide? Murder?

Perhaps it's silly but these questions plague her, so Crockett knocks on her neighbor's door and she asks if he might have a bike she can borrow. He knows all about Crockett's home life—he's heard it through the thin walls of her house at night—and he says yes, he has one. Yes, she can use it to go to the library. This poor girl all alone and all she wants to do is go to the fucking library.

Crockett hasn't been on a bike in years and her purse almost keeps getting stuck in the spokes. By the time she gets there her butt hurts and the muscles of her legs are thumping. Her armpits are wet and the nape of her neck is too. There is a different woman at the reference desk, but she finds the book easily enough: it's the only book on loan.

Crockett sits at a big table occupied by an elderly man with too many newspapers. She opens *Wonders of the East*.

Marvels Described by Friar Jordanus tells her about a smelly whirlpool in Italy, a flower that is a river in Greece. In Armenia the mountain where Noah's ark rested. Armenia where three Apostles were martyred. Armenia with its heathens now converted. In Persia worms that make honey. In India fruits as large as people. In India, cats with wings like bats. In India, ants with teeth. In India, dragons, unicorns, snakes with horns, men with dog heads. In Ethiopia gryphons.

Among these creatures, idolatrous people too. Dirty people. Funeral customs. Behavior. Eating. Those who have yet to be civilized. Those who are not Christian. Stones. Plants. Herbs. Colors. An entire chapter devoted to the size of these ancient nations. How one might travel from place to place.

And then it is the end. An appendix without the words *hen*, *chicken*, *exploding*.

"Excuse me," Crockett says to the new woman manning the desk.

"I think there's been a mistake with this book. It's supposed to say something about exploding chickens and there's no exploding chickens in it." She explains the problem and the woman is searching her computer, smiling, laughing to herself.

"Do you use Wikipedia?" the woman asks.

"No."

"You don't use Wikipedia? I thought all students use Wikipedia."

"I don't use it."

"Well, it says here that there are different versions of *Wonders of the East*. Can I see that?"

Crockett hands the book back over and the woman turns through the pages.

As Crockett waits, she realizes that she doesn't feel disappointed. She's not angry either that this might be the wrong book. Really, she feels nothing.

Crockett is used to nothing, the vague recognition of a hole where something should go. She feels the edges of the hole, knows something is being sucked down into it when she watches TV, sees bright houses on flat, green lawns. When her sister calls from college to announce she's won another scholarship. When her mother enters the house with another man on her arm. When tests are passed back and there's always a C, or D, or F. When Andy Johnson calls and says *hey, a bunch of us are going to sneak into the pool* and shows up at her house but there is no one else, just Andy Johnson and a fifth of vodka. When in the middle of the night she wakes and her door is open and Greg Monce is standing there, backlit by the TV. These feelings get sucked down too fast for her to even know what they are.

Her mom told her once, "Jesus will fill you up. Fill you with light." But Jesus was a carpenter and not a county road crew worker. And carpenters don't fill holes. They just cover them up. Crockett wonders why

Jesus wasn't a man who patched potholes, or if they didn't have potholes back then, why he wasn't a grave-digger. They fill holes too.

"Well I don't think this is a translation of the version you want," the woman breaks in.

Crockett doesn't understand.

"I think what you want is the *Beowulf* version. I can get that for you too."

"Would this help?" Crockett digs in her purse and pulls out *Adeline's Farm for Exploding Chickens*. There's a wrapper stuck in the pages, and when she pulls it off, old gum comes with it.

"Where in the world did you get this?" The woman has never seen the book, which she says isn't surprising because you'd never believe how many books there actually are.

"My sister found it. It's self-published."

"Oh." The woman turns pages in this book too, laughs some more. "Unless there's a footnote or some appendix, I don't know what to tell you. You want a different book?"

Crockett takes it back. "No. Thank you though."

She goes to a computer and types in "Adeline's Farm for Exploding Chickens."

Explosion at Bay Bridge Facility Kills 4. Patients Recover after OSHA. There is one result in the middle that might be it.

When Crockett clicks on the link, she's taken to a YouTube page titled "Commercials You'll Never Believe Existed." She presses play.

*

Ma spends most of the time in the barn. *Her* barn.

She's painted the walls white, but the lumber is old and untreated so the paint job looks awful. Country-chic, she calls it. And maybe if this wasn't a farm, and we had money, and it was all intentional, it would look good. Maybe in a house with a pool, fountain, and big glass windows it would even look classy.

Instead, it's a barn. In summer it makes me sweat. In winter it's freezing. I can see through the slats of the wood to the chicken coops outside and it smells like straw and dust.

In the loft, ma has set up her dressing room. Her mirrored vanity is against the wall, her little white chair always pulled out. Putting on her face. Cold-creaming it off. Mascara. Lipstick. Eyeliner. Tissue. Her makeup never looks right because *the curtains are too heavy and the light isn't good*. I don't tell her there are no curtains, no windows. The drapes she used to have are long gone, as gone as the apartment in Beverly Hills. She's got a bulb hanging from its wire. In its shadows are monsters made of gowns.

She doesn't even come into the house anymore. Three times a day I bring her food—breakfast and lunch and dinner—and she thanks me the way you'd thank a man in catering: a smile, no eye contact, a dismissive wave. Sometimes she'll ask my opinion on what dress she should wear: the one with the turquoise sequins, the one with the pink feathered hem, the crushed velvet mermaid. I like these times though because I can actually sit and talk with her, even if it's about old dresses. I don't tell her the sequins are falling off. I don't point out that feathers are obviously missing. I don't say that the crushed velvet has been eaten through by mice.

There are no dinner parties to go to. There are no award ceremonies. This is not Hollywood. This is Texas.

Today she's lying in bed in her dressing gown, a gauzy mauve with lace at the collar. She's looking at the TV. It isn't on but she says, "Isn't Humphrey Bogart the best?"

She's "watching" *The Maltese Falcon* again.

"What part are you at?" I ask, setting down fried eggs and toast on her night stand.

"They're talking about the black bird," she says, and then begins to whisper memorized dialogue to herself.

"Ma," I say, "I've been thinking…"

She leans over, reaching for a piece of toast, still mumbling.

"You know grandpa isn't doing too well. He says he's worried about you in here all day, especially at night with the chickens. What happens if one gets frightened in its sleep? Bad chicken dreams? You're up here in the loft and if it catches fire…"

She isn't listening. What do you say to a person who won't listen? You don't say, *remember how your ma died? Remember how ugly she was before she did? All burned up with scars on her arms? Remember how grandpa loved her, ugly as she was? Remember how what you look like doesn't matter in the end when you're dead and in a casket because you scared a chicken and it took your legs?*

"I was thinking it's time to sell the farm," I say instead.

Ma responds, but not to me. She's in a memory, a dream, someplace that is not her barn. "Remember when we went up to that big house in the hills? That was the night I landed my first role."

"No, ma, *we* didn't go."

"Don't be silly. You remember how the director said, 'that's not a woman's lines' but laughed because he could tell I could play any role. I was that good. A female Humphrey Bogart. A black bird."

"Black bird is dead ma, remember?"

The black bird all covered in pink guts and red blood blown to bits by some tourist honking his horn. Black bird and my grandma's black skin: singed by the explosion. One leg beside her, the other blown clear off into the chicken pen.

"Alright, then," she says, steeling herself with resolve come from nowhere.

"Really? You want to sell the farm?"

My ma shakes her head, toast forgotten in her hand. "We can't sell the farm," she says. "It's how I got my start."

*

Crockett sits on the sofa reading her book. She wants to finish the story, of course, but she also wants to forget the time. Her heart starts to thump when she hears tires on the gravel outside, a door closing, her mother laughing.

The screen door squeaks open. And there is her mother. Denim cut-offs, cowboy boots, Ponytail. Greg behind her with the suitcases, smacking the door frame with them. Her sister behind him, quiet.

Her mother has brought Crockett something. A picture of her and Greg Monce at an aquarium, posed in such a way that a shark looks like it's about to eat them. She's also brought Crockett a magnet which she uses to put the picture on the refrigerator.

"I know I should be wide awake with the time change," her mother says, "but I'm dead beat."

"Crockett," Greg Monce says.

She nods at him.

"Why don't we take a shower," he says to her mom, and her mom giggles.

Alone with her sister in the kitchen, Crockett feels that hole again, gaping open. Something slipping.

"I'm gonna head back," Crockett's sister says, not looking at her.

"What? Now? It's dark."

"Yeah, but…"

"You can't leave."

"I got work and school's gonna start soon. I have things to do."

"Fine."

"Look, Crockett, just hang in there."

"You gonna even say goodbye?"

"I already did."

Crockett's sister doesn't even ask for the book. She just puts her stuff in a duffel bag and goes out the door.

In the bathroom Crockett hears her mom laughing. Hears her mom call "Croooooock-ettttt? Are there any towels?"

Crockett picks up the phone. She calls Andy Johnson. She says, "I need to get out of here."

*

"It doesn't make sense," I say to grandpa.

He's lying in bed, like my ma, but unlike her, he's not pretending to watch movies. He's dying.

"No one wants exploding chicken eggs. No one wants exploding chickens." Even after they took his wife he still won't let go. And now it's me, ma, and a bunch of chickens, and I don't want them either.

"Do you even know how hard it is to raise exploding chickens?" he asks me. His eyes are red and the lids are almost translucent. "How hard it is to even get them? How hard we worked to bring them up?"

He's not accusing me. I know he thinks I don't know, that I don't get it. And maybe I don't. I didn't spend seventy years here doing this. I've only been alive for fifteen.

But I can talk to grandpa in a way I can't talk to ma. I list all the reasons why we should sell the farm, the chickens. We barely get by. They're destroying property. Fire trucks can't get out here quick enough. Ma is goin' crazy in the barn. Grandma is dead.

"Some things are worth waiting for," he tells me.

"But what *are* we waiting for?" I ask.

"For her."

Mayhap it's too much to lose a wife and a daughter.

Later, when it's dark and the moon is full, I leave the house, leave the body of my grandfather, and go to the barn.

I'm careful with the door, careful not to startle the chickens. They're all piled up together in a corner. One big, wide mass in the dark: brown, white, grey. They move a bit, but not too much. They undulate, a thick blanket of feathers waving like tall grass.

My ma sits at the picnic table, an old script in her hands. The light from the loft isn't strong enough so she's lit candles and they're almost burned out, wax pooling on the wood. I sit down across from her.

"Ma. Grandpa is gone."

She's running her finger along the page, mouthing words. "Can you read this with me?" she asks.

She hands it over, the screen play for *The Big Sleep*.

"Ma, they already made this movie."

"Doesn't matter," she says. "It wasn't right that time. It can be made again."

"They're not going to do that, ma."

"Are you going to help me or not?"

"Ma, did you hear me? Grandpa is dead."

She shakes her hands across the table, reaching for the pages. "Then give me that; I can do this myself."

"I gotta call the cops. The doctor. Someone."

"Go go go." She gets up and starts walking towards the ladder up to the loft.

"You can't leave this wax here," I tell her, raising my voice. "The chickens will eat it."

"Won't hurt them."

"Grandpa is dead. Maybe it's time for you to come in the house."

She's already in the loft, pulling up the ladder behind her. It makes an awful racket and the chickens wake, start moving around.

"Ma, you can't do this."

"Tell it to my agent."

"You don't have an agent anymore."

The chickens are coming to the table, confused at why they've been woken. Time for breakfast, they think. They mill around it, hop up onto it.

Ma throws the script to the ground where it lands with a pop. In the corner there's a bang. The chickens are running, squawking, flapping. The base of the wooden wall is covered in chicken, but there's no fire, not this time. Just to make sure, I grab a bucket of chicken water and douse it. I hear a hiss and a sizzle.

"See what you made me do?" she asks, her head popped over the bottom of the loft.

Back inside the house I call the police. *There's a body*, I tell them. *You need to pick him up. But please, please, wait until morning. Wait until I can get the chickens in the cow pasture. And please, don't honk.*

*

When the motion sensor light comes on, I get off the sofa. Arthritis is flaring up again, but I manage to pick up the shotgun.

In the drive a truck has pulled up, turned off its lights.

No use pretending like I'm not here.

I open the door. "Whoever you are, you're not welcome here," I call. The dome light in the truck clicks on. I pump the gun. "This is private property."

In the car I can see two kids, a boy driving, a girl in the passenger seat. She's got a bag in her lap and she's talkin' to the boy, but I can't hear what she's saying. She opens the door wider, sticking one leg out. "Don't slam the door," I call.

She gets out, a little thing. She doesn't slam the door. She closes it gently, and even though I'm holding a gun she walks towards me, bag slung over her shoulder.

"Is this Adeline's?" she asks.

"Who wants to know?"

She fiddles with her pack and pulls out a book. My book. "Had a hard time finding it," she says, "in the dark. You know you're not listed anywhere."

"I know."

She stands there, between me and the truck. The motion sensor light goes off and then she's smaller than she was before. Without the light there's no curves. She could almost be a small boy. I wave the barrel of the gun in the air and the light comes back on. She's stepped back.

"You've come to see the chickens," I say, and she nods.

"Yes," she says, "I've come to see the chickens." She waves to the boy in the truck who starts it up. Turns on the lights. Blinds me with them.

"I thought you'd be... Younger," the girl says, stepping up onto the porch.

"Girl, ain't no one young around here but you."

"He knows to go slow," she says, "to be quiet."

And the boy does know this. He turns around and drives slow just like I would. Like grandpa taught me. "Well we gotta wait until morning," I say.

"But they're here? They're here?" The girl says this twice. Once a question. Once a plea.

I get people like her from time to time. People who've read my book, tracked me down. Normally they know not to show up in the middle of the night. People who've read my book know the middle of the night is not a good time for loud noises.

"Looks like you're planning to stay," I say.

She nods.

"Well, come on then. No point in loitering out here."

FOR THE CARING
OF CATFISH

The girl begins her day when it is still night. The house has quieted. The men have left and the Women are sleeping. The girl steps softly in her stocking feet so as not to wake them. She knows what boards are loose and which will sing like small birds. The house is riddled with these nightingale floors, built to warn of intruders or assassins. But the Women here do not worry about being killed; they worry about being found out. They keep their secrets closely guarded, and the girl lived here for five years before she was taught a quiet pathway across the floors.

She begins her day in the dressing room where lamps still burn. When the sun rises the maids will come and collect the robes and wash the counters. Before they do, the girl must remove the faces. These are hidden behind the girl's favorite screen. She wonders why the screen is squandered in the Women's dressing room, but knows better than to ask the house mother who will tell the girl it's not her place to question. The screen is a painted swamp. But it isn't murky, and the darkness of it is not foreboding or frightening; it is not a place where a fifolet might be lurking in the waters or behind rocks, waiting to mislead weary travelers. The swamp is painted in dark greens, greys and muted moss and thin browns, as if the colors had been watered down before being applied to the cloth. It isn't dark at all, the girl thinks—rather, it is light, ethereal, and even when the sun goes down with only lamps and candles to light the house, the screen remains a ghost, a wisp. Except for the orchids.

They nestle in the crooks of trees, in the thin, delicate splits of branches near the base. The orchids are in stark contrast to the rest of the screen: a violent match of purple and fuchsia for the almost swamp. The girl likes the orchids because they are out of place; they are vibrant and real. They belong and don't belong. They are a different type of beauty. She can't imagine the screen without the orchids. She can't imagine the orchids without the swamp. She is only able to distinguish the importance of each because of its complement. The girl wonders every day if beauty only exists because of comparisons.

Beauty is not the dry and brittle faces in the bottom of wooden buckets. These are tattered and by the time she arrives to collect them, they have begun to smell of rot. Perhaps they were beautiful at another time. There's no way for her to know. All she knows is that there is no beauty in decay. This is what she tells herself when she collects the buckets of discarded faces. She has to tell herself this in order to feel better. She is not an orchid in a swamp, timeless and irrevocable like the flowers on the screen. Neither is she a Woman, though she wants to be.

As she leaves the dressing room, she is careful with her bounty. The buckets are light, but if she were to carry them recklessly they might bump against each other and make noise. She thought to do this once, to save time, and one of the Women appeared in the hallway, her face darker than the shadows in the corners. The girl never did it again. Now she tells herself that caution is a form of beauty. She moves over floors like gentle water and pretends she is a princess who must escape her captors.

At the bottom of the path outside the house is a rickety dock and tethered to it, an old fishing skiff. She bends down to light the lamps hanging from the brow and bow. Already the pond's placid surface begins to tremble. She places the buckets under the bench and pushes off with a long pole, rows her way out to the middle of the water while the boat rocks side to side. She raps lightly on the wood with her knuckles. Below, the vibrations are felt by the catfish. They are scarred and large and the house mother told her that they've been here for hundreds of years. The girl hasn't the courage to ask whether the fish are here because of the Women or if the Women are here because of the fish. She suspects the latter.

She plunges her hands into the first bucket. The skin and paint has dried into a thin flake, though it doesn't fall apart easily. She must shred it into smaller bits, which she does, wondering to which Woman this face belonged. It feels warm in her hand and when she is done, she sprinkles it into the water. The catfish rise, and the fins of the tired monsters splash the surface. Their mouths are larger than her hands, but they are gentle. She sees their eyes rolling towards the moonlight. She empties the buckets, one by one, until the water around the boat appears to boil. She plants her feet firmly to the wood, bends her knees and rocks with the boat. The lamps make the water look like moonlit blood.

In the last bucket she finds a face that hasn't torn at all. In fact, it's warmer than the others, and still pliable. In five years this is the first time she's felt in her hands what it must feel like to wear one of the painted faces. It feels almost like skin, but somehow wetter, and heavier too. There are six Women asleep in their long beds. She knows whose face this is.

She holds the face up to the light and discerns the arch of the eyebrows, the bow of the colored lips. She knows this face must belong to Sabine, with arms and legs like willow branches. Below her, the fish grow impatient. The girl wonders why Sabine's face is so fresh, why it does not wilt like the others. She thinks of Sabine's slow movement when pouring bourbon and how she no longer covers her entire mouth when she laughs. She thinks of Sabine's knees edging closer to the young men she entertained after dinner.

Instead of shredding the mask, the girl rolls it and folds it into the pocket of her robe. She rows back to the dock, leaving the catfish still hungry and confused in the middle of the lake, imagining her own face painted, pliant, beautiful.

*

The girl overhears a piece of the puzzle: how to become a Woman.

"You must first accept that *you* are not important. *You* are an image, and a dream, something unobtainable. *You* are expectations and desires and *you* are an art to be created by the will of others."

The Woman with the fishtail braid is standing beside Sabine, who is crying, and the girl wonders if there can be tears if there is no face. The Woman shakes Sabine and tells her, not unkindly, that she is nothing.

The Women turn to see the girl in the room, the dirty clothes in her arms. They hiss like snakes and the girl leaves feeling like a ghost has touched her. Later, she wonders how long Sabine has been in the house, wonders whose cast-offs she is wearing while she cleans.

*

When the house mother summons the girl, at first she fears her theft has been discovered. The face is still whole and pliant and hidden in the pocket of winter clothes. Before she goes downstairs, she checks to make sure it is still there, and then she steels herself for dismissal.

The house mother is an older woman who does not paint her face. Her hair is coiled in elaborate ropes and the corners of her eyes are ribbed with deep lines. The girl is quiet when she enters, closing the door behind her and waiting with downcast eyes while the house mother finishes writing her letter. When the house mother is done, she folds her hands together and invites the girl to come closer.

The house mother tells the girl that she is to stay away from the Women. They are not to be disturbed, or admired. She is not one of them, yet.

The girl nods her head, her breath catching in her throat, escaping her lips, finally, in the demurest exhalation. *Yet.*

"Well then." The house mother evaluates the girl and does not like everything she sees. The girl is thin yes, and graceful, but her hair is a little coarse and she bites her nails. Her fingers are long and unknotted at the joints and there is potential in her voice, for as little as she uses it. She's an ugly thing, there's truth there, but a face doesn't matter for these Women.

She tells the girl she is nothing and if she's not more careful, she'll go back to sleeping in the bayou.

*

The girl does know she's not important, but she wants to be. This is why she dreams of the horrible Women. Who wants to live a life like clouds, floating quietly and expected to *be*? It is hard to be a child and know you're unwanted. She's pushed this knowing down until it is flat like paper and over this she's written her own history:

Her mother was a painter and her father was a furniture maker. This is how they met, when her mother saw the screen her father made, her parents touched hands and became the same space. But as with all stories of unwanted children, this one too had an unhappy ending. It was too little money, not too little love, that sold the girl off.

One day she imagines she will be walking delicately on the streets and she will see an old couple at dusk setting a floating candle into a river for their child. She will know their faces because of her own. Now she wonders how she will recognize her parents if her face disappears.

*

The night is still and outside the magnolia has stopped scraping against the wall of the house. The girl is counting the moon's steps and soon she will go to feed the fish. She tells herself, *this is a servant's work. Servants are merely tools. I am to be used.* She tells herself this because she's convinced this is how the Women think.

But she does not believe this.

Hanging in her winter jacket pocket is the mask. She finds it in the dark with deft fingers and unfolds it gently, as if she was opening a flower not yet ready to yield. It's lost its warmth but the color of the lips is hot like coals and her fingers tighten with the memory of hunger and snow.

Fingers trace edges of color and one day she will be drinking whiskey and unaware of the pain in sitting too long. She lays down on the bed and tells herself, *in being nothing, a Woman can be anything,* but this too is a lie. She drapes the mask upon her own face and her fingers become a brush for makeup. She wants to see the Woman she will become.

*

The days are marked with cooler air and the girl begins to see the changes, only part of which are hers.

Sabine no longer deposits her face in the bucket for the fish. When after weeks of less food the catfish become impatient, rocking her boat with impunity, not curiosity, the girl must fight off the urge to tell the house mother what's happened. If Sabine had a face, a real face, the girl knows she would meet pleading eyes to not reveal the secret. She thinks perhaps this is an opportunity: when Sabine fails to be a Woman, the girl will take her place. She repeats a mantra at night with a false face over her own and repeats the word *nothing* until she sees it behind her eyes.

*

Nothing is still something. The girl comes to know this as she watches the Women. She stands shadowed in the hallway outside the parlor. On the other side of the wall she hears the stories of factories and riots and illnesses without cures. These stories are speared by singing, and piano, and the scent of cigars. Sabine sits too close to her patron and whispers so that the girl cannot hear her.

*

How to become a Woman: You must not question; you must know expectations.

Sabine is in the house mother's room. The girl can hear the older Woman speaking firmly; she can hear Sabine saying *yes, yes*. But also, *what do I do when he expects me to love him?*

You cannot love, you are nothing. Nothing cannot love.

Yes, yes.

He may expect you to love him, but Women only meet expectations. They do not become them.

Yes, yes.

This is a warning, Sabine. Do not let yourself be something other than what you are.

*

The girl wraps herself in a thin robe and flinches when the floors creak under her feet. Above her, a Woman is walking too, and the girl hurries away with the buckets so she will not be seen. So she will not see them.

She is confused because the house mother is full of contradictions: nothing is nothing except for when it is something.

In the lake the oar hits something in the water and she turns to see an arc disappear under the surface. When it bobs back up, the olive colored catfish glistens in the moonlight. Fish cannot live forever, she tells herself.

Other catfish take the faces into themselves and knock the body of their peer about in the water. Fish are cannibals but these fish ignore death. It disgusts her, this bloating body. It unnerves the girl that the others are unconcerned, uninterested in it despite their dwindling food, that they go on with needs despite loss. She hauls the body of the catfish into the boat to bury it.

*

As she lies in her narrow bed with the mask over her face, the wind comes through cracks in the window and she begins to shake. She tells herself again the story of her birth. She omits the sound of splashing, the writhing body of a fish in her small hands, the smell of her mother like moss decaying.

She tells herself she is the daughter of a painter and a furniture maker. She is not the daughter of fish-farmers, poor and starving. No, wait, she is *nothing*. She must remember this.

*

One night Sabine is simply gone. She is not entertaining, which sometimes happens when a Woman is ill or unwell, but when the girl goes to clean the dressing room, Sabine's makeup and paints are empty and her hangers and her clothing have disappeared.

*

The house mother calls the girl. Tells her in one month, she will begin her training. *Sabine is not with us anymore*, she says, and the girl wonders where a Woman without a face goes. Does it matter, she asks herself later. Sabine was nothing. I am nothing. We are all nothing.

*

The girl remembers things someone once told her about catfish. *When it thunders, catfish bite well. Catfish can live for hundreds of years. If a catfish comes to know you, it might eat from your hand, or even take food from your lips.* These bits of knowledge strike her at odd times, an old pain that comes with twisting the wrong way when sweeping or leaning too far forward with a heavy pail of water. The girl tries to push these thoughts from her mind, but when she goes to the pond they rush upon her in cascading colors behind her eyes.

The fish are thinner, and she knows this is a bad sign. Fish are not like people to lose weight and gain it depending on the season. She thinks she should have left the dead fish in the pond; it was a mistake to bury it. Perhaps over time they would have eaten it. As the catfish scrape along the bottom of the boat, the girl sits with the empty buckets, clutching the oars.

She tells herself it's nothing. That the fish are nothing to worry about.

No, the girl corrects herself, *I am nothing.*

The fish are angry, and she rows quickly back to shore.

*

The dressing room begins to change. Something about Sabine's disappearance has rattled the house mother; she is effacing person and place now. The Women's notes, tacked to the wall, struck through with nails, are gone. All the makeup is now arranged in a similar manner; the girl cannot tell whose dressing table is whose. The first time she sees this, the unfinished feel of the room disturbs her. No more robes thrown over chairs. Stools fit snuggly under tables instead of pulled out at angles, ghosts of careless movement the girl would be expected to correct. No more trinkets hanging from rafters, closet doors pulled shut and inside, orderly clothes pressed and limp.

No one has said anything about this to her, so the girl stands numbly, not sure of what to do. The room is a canvas, waiting to be painted on.

The girl does not see the buckets. They used to be beside the desks, but no longer. She spies one in the empty space below a desk, and pulls out a stool to retrieve it. Her own reflection catches her eye.

There are no mirrors in the house except for in the dressing room. The girl suspects this is because the Women don't want to see their no-faces; they don't need reminders about what they were. They are nothing now. The girl hasn't looked at her own face in years, and now she sees that something isn't quite right.

She bends over the desk, squinting her eyes against the light of the oil lamps. She opens her eyes wide, then squints again. Over the years her lean face has sharpened. Before she looked hollow. Now she looks sculpted. She sits in a chair, resting her forearms on the wood and leaning forward. She can see the soft pads of her cheek bones, the way the tip of her nose is perfectly even with her nostrils. Her eyebrows don't need to be groomed; they are dark and rounded and upon closer inspection, no stray hairs. This is not the face she remembers: this is the face of her mother.

There is a memory she discovers now: her mother's lips forming words she does not comprehend. Her mother is telling her, *we have to eat them*, and in a bucket she carries small fish. The girl's stomach is hurting, from cold or hunger she can't remember. It was winter and the fish were slow and tired in the cold water, awakened from their hibernation by her mother's netted pole. The girl remembers thinking it was wrong to eat the fish; they were not food, but she did it anyway. She trusted her mother.

In the mirror the girl's face now looks sad and old. It is a face of regret. It is the face of memory. She knows now why the Women shun their faces; some things are too terrible to be reminded of.

Behind her the movement of the house mother: *we won't be needing your services anymore*, she says, and the girl nods her head. In the mirror her eyes go dark.

*

Being a Woman means forgetting, the house mother tells her. The girl sits on a low stool in an empty room overlooking the pond. The house mother has thrown the windows open against the rising sun. The girl shivers.

The girl has never been in this room before, a small space off the house mother's own quarters. In front of her sits the buckets with the

Women's faces. The house mother collected them herself that night, the girl's duties absorbed by someone who would not make mistakes, who would know a missing face and what it implied.

There are six buckets; five of which have bottoms littered with makeup and paint. The sixth bucket, set apart, is for the girl.

The house mother bends at the knees in front of the girl, sits on the floor facing her.

Are you afraid? she asks.

The girl is not afraid. Instead, she feels powerful. Something about this turns in her stomach, a fish squirming in her gut. She knows she shouldn't feel this way. She shouldn't feel anything. Nothing can't feel something. Still, here is the house mother, demanding and stern, on her knees. The girl feels a power shifting.

The house mother reaches up above the girl's ear where hair meets smooth skin. The girl watches the old woman expectantly. There is something in her face while she works, concentration, worry perhaps. The house mother does not know that the girl sees her biting her lower lip, that the corner of her mouth on one side is turned down. Her hands work nimbly, depositing pink and white skin into the bucket. The girl sees no blood, feels no pain. She feels nothing at all, as if the house mother was simply waving her hands in a slow motion.

When the house mother is done, her eyes are critical and sharp, but she rests back on her heels and nods her head. *Take this,* she says, handing the girl the bucket with her own face. *Let go when you can*, she says, and the girl knows what she means. *You are nothing*, she tells the girl, but the girl knows this is a lie. She is anything now.

*

The girl will not receive her face, or a name, until she heals. The house mother tells her this, and the girl must trust that she looks wounded. She is no longer allowed in the dressing room. The next time she enters it she will be a Woman.

The house mother arranges her in Sabine's old room. The closet is filled with slips and robes and silk stockings, and she feels shame when adding her own meager belongings. She hears the Woman with the fishtail braid in the hallway: *it's better not to keep the old things*, she says, and the girl knows she is right. Better not to have the memories. She begins to clear out her past, and then she comes to the winter jacket, and folded inside, Sabine's face.

Sabine's face has become crumpled. The once unlined mask is now creased, the makeup flaking off. The girl moves to throw it away, but remembers the fish.

*

At breakfast with the Women, the girl learns what it is like to be one of them. The Women appear as phantoms, sliding into the room in draped cloth, sitting in chairs with fluid movement. The girl has never been in their part of the house and did not know it was a prison. Their breakfast comes with a blind servant, someone the girl has never seen before but who clearly understands the house: her footsteps sure and knowing.

For the first time the girl can see clearly the Women's no-faces. They are not terrible like they used to be. She can see hints of facial features smoky in the darkness. What a nose might look like, the vague outlines of lips. The girl wonders what her own face looks like now, if it appears scabbed and caked or if there is soft black, nothing. They talk little; they eat in quiet. The girl wonders what they are expected to do all day.

*

From her high window the girl sees the pond, fog moving across the grass. She sits on her bed and looks down into the bucket. Her face is a tattered mess. It is shredded beyond repair. She does not want to look at it.

She wonders if this room has always been so bare or if it has been made blank just for her. She hates the sterility. *I am a Woman,* she thinks, remembering the house mother on her knees before her.

The boards sing under her feet. She does not know these hallways and as she explores the sound of birds follows her. She will need to re-learn her patterns, establish new ones. The rooms of the other Women are rather blank, and the girl is disappointed by this. She wasn't sure what she expected: luxury, comfort. Inside the room of the Woman with the fishtail braid, she sees the screen.

She had forgotten it, the screen with the swamp and the orchids. But here it is, opened against the closet doors, its flowers blossoming fiercely. It was her screen first, she thinks, angry at the theft. It should be in her room. *I am a Woman,* she thinks, and stands there a long time, looking first at the screen, then past the screen, where outside it has begun to rain.

She goes to find the Woman, the floor screaming under her harsh steps.

She enters the part of the house she knows, but she does not take the quiet path. Instead the floors trill all the way to the dressing room where she knows she'll find the other Women preparing for the night.

When she throws the door open the Women are startled. They've been so deep in work they did not hear her announcement. They are sitting at their tables, their bodies twisted and leaning away from the door she has just opened. Their faces are painted to look like hers. She remembers the bone structure and brows and nose and lips. They have taken her face.

Shhh, the raven-haired Woman's mimicking mouth says, beckoning the girl forward, pointing at the mirror. The raven-haired Woman stands up, pushing the chair back softly with no noise. The girl approaches, and can see now that the Woman's lips are slightly smeared, one eyebrow is higher than the other. They are practicing.

The girl looks in the mirror. What looks back is pink with black creeping in tendrils through the wounds. The raven-haired Woman smiles, revealing messy red paint on white teeth. The girl flees the room, trying to run as quietly as she can.

*

The house mother is at her writing desk and the girl slips by her room unnoticed. In the kitchen she collects rice and vegetable castoffs, cradling them against her breasts as if a small, starving child stealing food. She deposits these into the bucket with her face, and on top of these, the disintegrating remnants of what was Sabine.

Outside, water droplets pelt the girl's body. When she turns she sees the house mother, flanked by the Women, at the top of the path. The house mother is yelling, but her voice is lost in the wind and rain. She beckons for the girl to return.

The girl flees instead, her feet slipping on wet ground. She sets her bucket in the boat and begins to row. The oar hits something in the water. The girl's stomach feels like a stone and she doesn't want to look, knowing what she'll find.

The catfish seethe beneath her, unnatural and aggressive. She remembers what these fish should do, how they should be sleepy with cold in the depths of the pond. She plunges her hands into the bucket and then into the water. She feels their mouths like wet silk and they gum her fingers, eager for more food, eager for her.

She stands up, swaying in the boat, and then simply lets herself fall overboard.

The girl hopes the catfish will come for her, eat her up and absorb her the way they do the faces of the other Women, but they do not. They do not want live flesh. They do not want the girl who is not yet a Woman.

*

The house mother watches the girl who will not be a Woman, who will be forever half-formed, row with the buckets across the lake. A *shame*, the house mother thinks, tapping her nails on the glass, *she could have been something*. Instead the girl is nothing, but the house mother does not mourn the girl. If anything, it taught the other Women a lesson. No one wants to be a fish-feeder, the house mother thinks haughtily.

It is winter now, and the days are slow and tepid. The girl spends her days the way she used to, cleaning and straightening the dressing room that again has taken on its previous look. It was almost as if none of it ever happened, except for her face.

Tonight she rows out in the pond, but below the surface the fish are sluggish and only nibble algae. She unhooks one of the lamps and holds it close to the surface. She crumples the faces into flakes and holds them with her fingers under the water but still, no fish. She slaps the water with her hand in frustration. There is movement in the darkness, grey amid the black. The girl pleads, *come, come*, and tears settle in the corners of her eyes. She tells the fish she needs them, but nothing.

MORE ENDURING FOR HAVING BEEN BROKEN

When Emery stepped outside, he saw his mother watering the dirt again. Every morning at seven she uncoiled the hose hanging from the side of the trailer and wet the ground, the sand, the scrubby bushes. She said she had to drown the demons, all the Arizona bugs that masqueraded in carapace, and with wings, and with segmented bodies: forms that betrayed their true shapes. Water was the only way to keep them quiet. Fill their mouths and they'd choke and die. And then, eventually, they would shrivel up. Become husks. Break apart. Be absorbed by the good earth.

Emery let the door slam behind him and the silence between him and his mother was thin and hot. He passed her, wet red clay coating the sides and bottom of his no-name tennis shoes. The yard had fractured in sun after months of dry heat. In places, these fissures yawned for water and Emery imagined the insects below ground, the confusion and then, swift death from the water hose. It upset him and he fingered the money in his pocket. He'd been stealing a dollar every few days from his mother's purse for three months, and now he had fifty dollars of guilt money that he was eager to get rid of. Tommy Endelson had a California King snake without a tongue. The woman who sold it to him said the snake had lost it in a fight with another snake, and now Tommy was tired of his broken pet. Emery said he'd buy it off Tommy: snake, cage, wood shaving bedding, mice-cicles, everything he had, and Tommy said sure.

Tommy's trailer wasn't much nicer than Emery's, but Tommy did have a father who was almost seventy and still climbed mountains. It was this man that opened the door—the sound like a laughing dolphin—standing with a cup of coffee in one hand.

"Hey Buck," Emery said, "Tommy home?"

Buck shook his head. He looked like a snow peak in shadows standing there in the doorway, grey hair flowing to his shoulders. He pointed to the hills with his mug. "Went out to the castle. Aren't you boys supposed to be in school anyway?"

Buck and his son Tommy had different last names, and one of the reasons Emery and Tommy were friends was because Emery's mom believed in demons and Tommy's father looked like aged leather: neither parent fit in. Buck also had a tendency to forget things, like the length of summer vacation and to pay the water bill.

"How long ago?" Emery asked.

Buck lowered his mug, raised it, swung it back and forth and coffee sloshed out. A dowsing rod for time and children. "An hour maybe?"

"Okay, because I was supposed to buy his snake."

"Chipper?"

Emery hated the name Tommy had given the snake and was still contemplating a much better one. "Yeah," he confirmed.

"Well I'll bundle him up and drive him over for you."

"Thanks, Buck. I'm going to go find Tommy."

Emery still had his hand in his pocket. The money was becoming soft with sweat.

*

The castle was what the local kids called the cliff dwellings. They'd learned about them in school and also learned that the Barnoff family owned the land *and* owned the dwellings. Upon the most recent Mr. Barnoff's death, the land would finally be donated to the government and there were already plans for making it a national monument. That was fine with Emery. The children had also learned that all the hiking up the steep hillside, the illegal tourists and artifact dealers, had been eroding the seven-hundred-year-old limestone complex. That didn't stop Emery and the other local kids from going up there, though. They didn't see themselves as part of the destruction.

It took thirty-two minutes of brisk walking to reach the castle from the trailer park. When Emery finally emerged from the footpath, Tommy was at the base of the dwellings, practicing his ninja moves.

"Tommy!" Emery called, and the other boy's head whipped around. He was holding the severed spine of a yucca plant—a Spanish Bayonet, Buck told them once—and he was oddly small against the rising cliff-face behind him. This was the first time Emery had ever seen anyone below the dwellings alone, and that complex, three stories high and shaded by a natural overhang, was massive above, almost threatening. Emery knew that the ceilings of the dwellings were less than five feet tall and that at almost five feet, he had to hunch to walk through the rooms. He was not sure if people who had lived there were small enough to walk around without scalping themselves, or if they were constantly bent over while inside. At home once, he did an experiment where he walked around hunched for a few hours and then his neck and lower back hurt. He imagined the people who used to live in the dwellings had a painful life.

"Hey!" Tommy called, wielding his sword.

Emery jogged up to him, still breathing hard from the uphill walk. Before he reached the other boy, he had the money out, folded in half, sharp crease at the middle, arm outstretched. "I got the money," Emery said.

Tommy let his sword arm drop. He didn't take the money, and Emery was scared that Tommy was going to backtrack and decide to keep his snake.

"Saw some guys out here earlier," Tommy said. "Taking pictures and stuff. They said we can't be here anymore, but I told them they weren't the cops and they didn't have a warrant."

"Who were they?" Emery still had the money between them, exchange struggling across the canyon.

"Forest rangers or something."

"Oh."

"Yeah, they said they didn't need a warrant and that I apparently didn't know what one was, and that they'd make sure no one messed with the place. But they left and I'm still here, so whatever."

Emery was tired of straining and he shook the money at Tommy. He knew the gesture looked frantic, made him look desperate. "Fifty dollars," he said. And then, as if his claim was staked and irrevocable, "Your dad's packed him up and taken him to my house."

"Oh yeah, okay, sure." Tommy took the money. Didn't count it. Just shoved the wad unceremoniously into his pocket.

Emery wasn't sure if he was happy or sad. He felt guilty for stealing from his mom; he didn't know if he wanted the manifestation of it to be discarded or treasured.

Tommy kicked the purple fruit off the top of a prickly pear cactus and then crushed it underfoot. "I'm gonna buy something really cool," he told Emery. "There's a bike for sale at the gas station and I'm going to get it."

Emery didn't care what Tommy did with the money as long as *he* got the snake. California King snakes were immune to Rattlesnake venom and could even eat them. Emery was impressed by this, and would rather have a wounded predator than none at all. He was eager for Tommy to leave, spend the money, seal the deal, but the other boy was playing oblivious to Emery's anxiety and wouldn't budge.

"You want to help me practice? Before it gets too hot?" Tommy held up his bayonet and waved it like a wand.

Emery didn't want to practice Tommy's ninja moves. It annoyed him that Tommy attempted a warped type of martial arts with a fake Spanish sword. Tommy's movements were rash and explosive. When they had taken martial arts together last year, their instructor was calm and fluid and every move he made melted into the next and his body was a river.

"Okay," Emery relented, and Tommy rushed him, piercing his left arm with the sharp plant, a small red spot exploding from his skin.

*

Emery scrambles up the side of the rock and he hears the word *loser* being yelled at him. His arms are scratched like railroad tracks and his right eye is swelling, but he finds the hand and foot holes he needs and climbs up and up, scraping his stomach over the sill of a hard-baked entrance, tumbling inside the castle.

He sits like this until the laughter and curses stop, and when Emery pulls his head up from the cool darkness, there is no one below. The opening he peeks out of is an awkward height. Standing, Emery's nose is pressed against the ancient clay, breathing in musty dust and centuries, his eyes just clearing the edge. It might have been a door, or a window, maybe some odd type of lookout hole. The ceiling slopes down father into the dwelling; where Emery stands is the only place he can remain completely upright.

He is on the second floor of the dwelling, and he's forgotten how dark and still it is inside. The small openings throughout the complex are strategically placed for a cross breeze, but Emery knows if fires were lit, the interior would be heavy with smoke. He'd done that once too, hauled up dry twigs and leaves and one of his mom's lighters and tried camping when she was going through one of her difficult spells. He'd been smoked out and returned home defeated and smelling of campfire.

The room is dusty. There are no footprints on the floor and Emery wonders how long it has been since anyone climbed up. The teenagers prefer to drive to the next town over and park for hours at Sonic; when they sneak off to make out it is in the caves near the river, which is really more of a brown and sluggish creek. The castle is a dying place, inhabited occasionally by trailer park kids who have to find their own fun, who can't buy it.

Emery's face throbs. He and the castle are the same thing, beaten and broken, only no one is coming to save Emery. His mother is at work at the diner and when she comes home she will be frightened by the way he looks, and then she will be angry, and he will go to sleep with the sound of the TV too loud, and the next morning he'll wake up to the sound of water pelting the metal siding of the trailer.

Only tonight, there will be the snake. When Emery is in his room the snake will be there like some sure king and at least one thing will be different and bright. Maybe if he waits long enough, his mother will be asleep by the time he gets back.

*

Emery spends the day in the castle, moving like wind through the rooms, all three floors some split-level dream, napping on the castle roof in the shade of the limestone overhang, scraping bat shit off the roof with his nails, wondering how many bats actually live in the castle now. He wonders when the rangers will come back, if it will be later today and if, when they find him, they'll write him a ticket, or worse, arrest him. This fear nags at him until he decides it will be better to face his mother than to go to jail.

He climbs down the narrow stairs to the first level, to the largest opening, but movement catches his eye near the doorway. It is a red velvet ant, what he knows is actually a wingless female wasp, winding a looping path in the sunlight towards the shade. It almost looks like a black widow in a funhouse mirror. Its head, thorax, and legs are black and fuzzy, its abdomen an orange-red. Emery remembers the time he found a black widow hanging in its web from the rusting pipe play set behind their trailer. He had liked the color combination, the red set into the black, and had shown his mother, who doused the spider in Raid spray.

The red velvet ant is about half an inch long and Emery crouches down on his heels to get a better look. Why the female wasp is called an ant, he doesn't understand. Adults are supposed to be the smart ones, the correct ones. How hundreds if not thousands of people could be misled by one wrong word escapes him. A red-tailed hawk's feathers are more brown than red. Buck told him once that in the *Odyssey*, the ocean is referred to as *the wine dark sea* but that wine isn't blue. Buck told Emery that our perceptions of color and material changes over time and that the ancient Greeks didn't even have a word for the color blue. Emery now wonders if the Greeks had a word for the color red, and if they did, if there might be more than one.

Emery sees the ant leaving many small lines in the dust, a cryptographic script by legs. He can almost see the words. They could be Latin, he thinks, or Greek, though he's never seen either language. But he does know the understanding is almost there. He is the snake without a tongue and cannot quite discern what is hiding.

The ant—wasp, Emery corrects himself—is now at the base of a wall and begins to climb up it. It arcs along until it disappears into a crack in the adobe that Emery didn't notice. He scrapes his feet in the dust and shuffles toward it, careful not to smear the insect's language. He looks out the door again, imagines his mother arriving home in the Plymouth, her careful steps across the front yard, her eyes searching for red velvet ants, her hurried hand twisting a key.

Emery begins to kick in the wall. He knows this place is sacred to someone, maybe not now, but it was, and he knows soon enough he won't be allowed to hide in the castle anymore. He decides he'll make his mark anyway. No one will ever know it was him. He will be invisible and permanent.

The last of the dried mud from his shoes is kicked loose and it crumbles to the ground where it's coated with dust from the shaking wall. Emery fears for a moment that he might bring the whole thing down the cliffside, that they'll find him buried in it days from now, a modern king in a castle grave, but then decides he doesn't care. He continues to kick and the crack lengthens, small gap broadening, and he kicks until the wall breaks in and there is darkness and ash beyond.

It is a small chamber, four feet by four feet, and in the center is a prickly pear cactus, its oblong purple fruit erupting from the pads. Emery knows plants don't grow where there is no sun, but the sun is setting and the room is dark and it is too strange to explore when there is no light. He vows to come back in the morning, when perhaps some small shaft will reveal itself.

He treads home, dusty and beaten. His mother's car is parked next to the trailer and the porch light is burned out. He climbs the stairs and almost kicks the snake's glass cage in.

Chipper is wound around a rock, and Emery can see a piece of paper taped to the top of the cage.

Take the snake back.

It is his mother's handwriting, beautiful and composed like a scribe's, and Emery feels like his eye is more swollen than it is, like the red wound on his arm that he knows is too puffy is over his heart instead.

He should have seen this coming, and he knows it.

Emery goes inside. His mother is in front of the television and Emery, instead of arguing with her, gets a flashlight from the kitchen drawer and lets the front door slam shut. He turns it on and looks into the cage, the snake black and cream in the light. He puts the note in his pocket. The bag of now thawing mice-cicles is on the ground, and Emery loops the handles over his left hand. He opens the cage, balancing the flashlight between his chin and shoulder, and lifts the snake out.

It is smooth and soft and shining and calm. It is smaller than he remembers it being, around three feet long, and it moves slowly between his hands. Emery notices two bulges in different places on its body. Herniated muscles, he remembers, from fighting with that other snake.

He drapes the snake over his neck, turns off the flashlight, and begins walking.

*

On the way to the castle the snake is a strange weight. It moves over his body but never attempts to escape him. It does not try to crawl into the bag with its food. It circles a path around him in the same language of the wingless wasp and again, Emery can *almost* decipher the words. At one point he is sure the snake has spelled *RED*, but the feeling of words on his body is too different from writing words on paper and he wavers in this knowledge.

In the sky, he can see the crescent moon over a mesa, a shark fin at the surface, and remembers his teacher telling the class that at one point, Arizona was under water. During the Paleozoic era, Arizona was an ocean, but Emery cannot remember if this is when megalodon lived. He knows that the scorpions he cannot see, small brown and black ones, had ancestors that were eight feet long and lived at the bottom of the ocean. It was so dark at those depths that the scorpions would flash phosphorescence to attract mates. Snakes too might have come from the ocean, evolving from an aquatic lizard, and Emery wonders if his snake and a Gila monster would ignore each other, fight, or silently accept their common origins in the ocean that used to drown this land.

Even when Emery reaches the base of the castle the snake is still calm and steady, unhurried and unconcerned. Emery climbs the dark rock face. He knows he should pay attention, look for scorpions and snakes that hunt in the night, but this California King is not worried, so maybe Emery shouldn't be either. The plastic bag rips and Emery has to tuck his shirt into his shorts and carry the plastic-sealed food against his stomach. The snake winds its head into Emery's sleeve and hesitates against his collarbone before emerging at the neckline.

In the castle, it is darker than Emery could have imagined. He looks out the doorway and sees the stars, the Milky Way. Small bats dive, profiled against the sky, and when Emery switches on his flashlight and shines it in their direction, they are like dark comets bombarding heavily towards the ground.

The snake becomes very still and rests its head in the crook of

Emery's arm. The flashlight illuminates the floor and Emery sees that he's tracked a path across the wasp's language. He feels this loss like hot stones behind his eyes.

He carries the snake into the small room. It stays pressed against him, warm and relaxed, as Emery searches with the flashlight for where sunlight might come from. As he does this, lines begin to appear on the walls and as he looks closer, he realizes there are drawings in the small chamber. They are thick and unsteady and when Emery stands back to take in the whole room, twisting the glass of the flashlight's lens to take it all in at once, there is *color* in the dark.

The cactus is the color of pine needles, the fruit is darker at the top than the base, white bubbling into pastel eggplant. The drawings are words he still doesn't know, in cobalt blue and burnt orange and tea-rose pink and red—dozens of red velvet ants escaping this nebula and taking their red dwarf bodies into a hole in the adobe near the cactus.

Emery pulls the snake from his body, gently, and places it on the floor of the room. He peels back the plastic around the thawed mice, and he places them next to it. The snake wraps around the dead bodies. Perhaps to protect its food. Perhaps to protect the memory of what lived.

Emery waits for a solid hour, willing the snake to extend its fork tongue, to taste this place and tell him in some small way that it understands. But the snake doesn't do this, and Emery has to tell himself that it knows. Knows this new home, knows it doesn't need a stupid name, knows it doesn't need a tongue and that injury does not constitute inability to thrive, and it knows that he's going to leave it and never come back.

The snake remains impassive, dark eyes that seem to be seeing everything but nothing at the same time, and Emery leaves the room, leaves the castle, and begins his walk home.

FICTIONS WE TELL OURSELVES

Outside the moving van is pulling up. The ramp is coming down. Men are approaching the door.

Meg's little brother, Jason, has his nose smashed against the window, breathing out through his mouth to fog the glass. Meg thinks he looks like a pig, and she says so. Jason turns and sticks his tongue out at her.

"Meg," her mother says sharply, "I want you to walk down with Jason to CVS. You remember where it is?" She pulls a twenty-dollar bill from her purse. "I can't have you two under my feet right now."

Of course Meg remembers where the drug store is. It is at the end of the block Charlie Tucker lives on, and Meg has a crush on Charlie Tucker. She's already planned on running into him there all the time.

"C'mon, turd," Meg says.

"You can't call me that." Jason follows her anyway, out the door and past the boxes amassing on the curb. "I don't like this house," he adds. "It smells like someone *died* in there."

"Shh!" Lowering her voice as they pass two men laboring with an armoire, Meg lies, "you'll frighten the movers away. Someone *did* die in there."

Jason becomes very quiet, and after a moment, reaches for Meg's hand.

*

The house they're moving into is in the same town they've been living in all their lives. It's even in the same sub-division, albeit on the other side. The new house is smaller and closer to school. No one wanted to leave the old house except for their mother who had closed doors and unplugged lamps and yelled at Meg and Jason when they needed to go into their father's study for computer paper or pens. Sometimes when their mother wasn't home, Meg would go into the study when she didn't need anything at all and just sit on the carpet and stare at books and the empty desk.

The school counselor had pulled Meg aside the week after the accident. In the woman's office, stuffy with the too-sweet scent of lilacs, the counselor had tipped her head to the side and told Meg how sorry she was. *Was there anything she could do*, she asked.

Meg wanted to say, *bring back my father*, but she knew how absurd the request would be. No one could bring her father back. So instead she tapped the soles of her feet on the carpet, looked at the sun coming through the window in an effort to burn the tears out of her eyes, and told the counselor no, she was dealing with it.

Have you cried? the woman asked, and that's when Meg snapped.

You don't know me, she almost yelled. *You have no right to be asking these questions.*

After that the counselor recommended help "outside of school," and Meg knew the woman wasn't prepared to be a real counselor, to actually deal with students' problems. Meg explained this to her mother—that the counselor was just pushing her buttons because it was her job—and Meg's mother, for some reason, believed her.

Looking back on it, Meg decided it was just easier for her mother to think only one child was taking it all so hard. She could deal with Jason's tantrums, his outbursts, his hitting the walls and throwing cups. She wouldn't be able to deal with Meg acting out too. And so Meg pretended she was working through it. And she was still pretending, right through the family dinner in which their mother told them she was selling the house—the place Meg had grown up in with him—right through the packing of his clothes, right through the donation bags of her father's now "give aways," because Meg had lost one parent, and saw too, on nights when her mother thought she was asleep upstairs, how she was on the edge of losing another.

*

It isn't until they're inside CVS that Jason broaches the subject of the death in the house. "How do you know someone died in there?"

"I wasn't even supposed to say anything. If mother finds out I told you she's going to be so mad."

Lately their mother has been prone to bouts of crying and swearing. She always apologizes, blames it on the stressful move. *Then why are we doing this?* Meg had asked her. *Because we have to,* her mother replied, but Meg didn't know if her mother meant there were money problems or if maybe the old house was just too much for her to deal with. This new, unpredictable mother made Meg uneasy. At times it felt like she didn't know her mother at all.

Meg and Jason are in the household goods aisle. She knows they need candles—the electric company had a mix-up and they have no AC, no lights—but she does not have enough money to buy the big candles in glass jars with names like Ocean Romance and Lily of Love. They are fifteen dollars each.

"I won't say anything." Jason is pulling her hand, begging for more information.

"Fine. Fine. But you have to *swear* on the grave of Floppy Ears."

When Meg and Jason were both younger this was the most serious of promises. Floppy Ears succumbed to a coyote and when Meg and Jason discovered his backyard hutch torn open with the rabbit's head in their mother's flower garden, it had given them nightmares for weeks. They took his death hard. The images—vivid and bright—were the most gruesome thing they'd ever seen.

"I swear I promise," Jason said.

"Okay." Meg selects tapered candles from different boxes: red ones and white ones and green ones and yellow ones. "But don't say I didn't warn you. Our house used to be owned by a family like ours. There was a mother, a daughter, and a son. The family had moved from Alaska to Texas when the father died—an oil well accident. But it wasn't long until the little boy started to hear voices in the walls. They told him to do things like take baths and brush his teeth. Eat all his vegetables and do his homework. Then one day when the boy heard the voice, he knew it was his father. He called and said, *Dad, Dad where are you?* And the dad said, *Trapped in the wall.* The boy looked all over the house, and he found a small door under the stairs. He'd never seen the door before, but behind it he could hear his father crying *It's so dark*, and so he opened it and went inside to find his father. But he never came back out. Because there was no door. No one could figure out how the boy disappeared. Where he went. A month later they found his body because the house had started to smell and the police brought in those dogs that sniff out dead people. They had to tear the wall down to get to him. You should pick something out," Meg tells Jason. "We got…" she counts the candles, factors in money for a Coke and a candy bar for herself, "five dollars."

Jason will not let go of her, even when Meg tries to switch hands holding the basket. "Is our house haunted?"

"Maybe," Meg says. "I guess we'll see. We probably don't have to worry though. I've heard ghosts aren't mean unless… No. I shouldn't say."

She is pulling Jason to the toy aisle. It is full of discount oddities: badly crafted knock-off Barbies called Brendas, oversized plastic Slinkys, tie-dyed stuffed animals, ping pong paddles with no balls. "What do you want?"

"No, tell me," Jason whines. "I need to know."

"You gotta swear."

"I swear on Floppy Ears."

"Ghosts don't get mean unless they were murdered. Unless they were killed by someone. And now you have to swear never to mention this again."

Jason looks as if he's going to ask a question. He opens his mouth but then closes it. He nods his head.

"What do you want? A water gun? What about this?" Meg looks down into a box of finger traps.

Jason shakes his head. Uninterested in the finger trap, he eyes little green plastic men with rubber-banded parachutes on their backs.

"No, these are great. I used to have one." Meg puts down the basket and picks up one of the finger traps. "You do it like this." She puts one finger in and then, looking down at the other hand still secured by her brother, says, "I need my hand to show you."

Jason lets go and Meg's hand is warm and wet with sweat.

"Okay, the other finger goes in here." Now Meg's hands are connected by the tube of interlocking strips. "See? Stuck." She tries to pull her fingers out, but the tube narrows. "But…" Meg, with great flourish, frees one finger. "Ta da! Here, you try."

Jason puts his arms out, but instead of pointing his fingers to receive the finger trap, he's cupping his hands, like he's offering something invisible. Meg separates his pointer fingers then works them into the finger trap. Jason tries to pull his fingers apart but can't.

At the cooler Jason is still working, still pulling, and Meg selects two cokes and a king-sized snickers bar. She lingers in the aisles, looking at scented shampoo and shaving cream—the latter which she doesn't even need yet—but there is no sign of Charlie.

"How do I get it off?" Jason finally asks. "Meg, how do I get it off?"

"You just gotta work at it. I did it, didn't I?"

*

Hours later, one of the movers shows Jason how to push instead of pull and how to hold the finger trap in order to get his fingers out. The sun is going down and the house is beginning to darken. The windows are open, but the house is stuffy and damp. It smells like wood and paint and stale piss and over that, their mother's perfume. There are boxes everywhere and the family eats pizza at the dining room table. Their mother has punched holes in Styrofoam cups and turned them upside down, wedging the tapered candles into them. Only after she does this does she realize she has no matches and catches one of the movers who happens to have a lighter that he gives to her. It makes her cry and the men leave quickly afterward.

"They'll come first thing in the morning," her mother says, but Meg realizes her mother is talking to herself about the electric company, not talking to Meg. Meg is trying to read *The Golden Compass* by candle-light and Jason is disassembling the finger trap, pulling apart the colored strips one by one, like unweaving a basket.

Before they go upstairs to sleep, Meg sees Jason pause at the landing, peeking around the banister. The wall under the stairs is flat and white: no door.

"What are you doing?" Meg asks.

"Listening," Jason replies.

"C'mon," their mother says, offering Jason an upside-down cup with a candle in it. "Walk slowly so the flame doesn't go out." Outside his bedroom she says *damnit* when they see she's forgotten to put sheets on the bed.

Jason's bedroom is on the right; Meg's is across the hall on the left. Jason had wanted the left bedroom because that bedroom had a sloped ceiling and a window seat, but Meg had gotten it because she was older and because she said the window seat made a perfect place for reading.

Meg looks into Jason's room, the twin bed, the boxes. "You know, I think this might have been *his* room."

"No, he would have wanted the *good* bedroom." Jason is backing up into the hallway, refusing the space allotted to him. "I'm not ready to go to bed," he adds.

"He probably had this room because he had an older sister, too," Meg says, ignoring her brother's last comment. "Besides, we can't always get what we want."

Their mother returns with one flat sheet, a comforter, and a pillow. By candlelight, Meg thinks her mother looks like a skeleton. Her cheeks look sunken and her eyes are too deep in her head. The shadows fall in all the wrong places.

"Mom…" Jason begins.

Meg looks at her brother. Nods her head and puts her finger to her lips. Widens her eyes. *Don't tell*, she says silently.

"Yes?"

Jason pauses. "Is there a night light?"

"No, sweetie. There's no electricity."

"Oh. Okay."

Jason's pajamas have not been unpacked so he gets into bed in just his underwear. "I don't like this house," he tells his mother as she tucks him in. "It's wrong."

"You'll get used to it," she tells him. "I've lived in lots of different houses. They always feel wrong at first. Once we get everything unpacked, you'll see. Do you want me to open the window? Try to get a breeze going?" she asks before she leaves.

Jason nods yes.

"I'll get my own sheets," Meg says, and leaves the room.

Across the hall, Meg looks out *her* window. She can see how quickly the clouds move across the moon. She can see the oak tree in the backyard and turns to face the wall instead, snuggling down into her quilt. She is almost asleep when she hears her door open. "Get out," she admonishes Jason, rolling over to face him, to give him her best angry face. But there is no one there. No Jason. No mother. When she gets up, she finds Jason asleep in his own bed, on his stomach, breathing deeply against his pillow. The streetlight outside flickers.

*

"Why don't you build a fort?" Their mother is unpacking the kitchen. Flattened boxes are stacking up. There are piles of cardboard around the house.

"A fort *inside*?" Jason is sitting at the breakfast table carefully unwrapping newspaper-covered plates.

"Why not? Meg can help you."

"Mother, I have things to do." Meg is still reading her book.

"Spend time with your brother. That's what families do. They spend time together."

Meg knows this is a lie. Their mother is always at a class—Pilates or pottery or some kind of yoga—and their father was rarely home. He spent all day at the law firm and at least twice a week their parents went to a dinner party or meeting or something that required an old babysitter who made them "clean their plates" even though Meg was clearly old enough to determine when she was no longer hungry.

"I'm sure I don't need to reiterate *how* important it is," her mother continues. "Look, there's tape on the counter. And scissors. You can draw on the walls and cut out windows."

"I can draw on the walls?" Jason asks.

"Of the fort," their mother clarifies. "Not of this house."

It's enough to interest Jason in fort-building. He's already out of the chair and dragging boxes into the living room.

"Mother." Meg puts down her book. "I'm not a kid."

"I know you're not. But your brother is and he's not getting along well in case you hadn't noticed. Did you know last night is the only night he hasn't crawled into bed with me the past three months?"

Meg did not know that, and so she stays quiet.

"You can do this *one* thing. For me."

"And what's anyone doing for *me*?"

"If you want to be treated as an adult you can act like one. Life is short and unkind and shit happens that fucks everything up and there's nothing to do about it but keep going." She slams the cabinet door. "They're not safety scissors," she says, not looking at her daughter. "Please."

*

In the living room, Jason has begun constructing the fort, but he does not know what he's doing. He's leaning boxes against boxes and trying to hold them in place but they keep falling down. They slide along the floor, send dust bunnies into the air. He's assembling the fort over the dark spots where someone's pet ruined the hardwood.

"You building a pueblo?"

"No. What's a pueblo?"

"Here, if we tape these it will hold them up." The tape gun in Meg's hands screeches as the tape is applied. Jason gives her directions: *it needs five rooms, six. Too large. Too small.* Meg cuts the cardboard and tapes it together. *There should be a window here.* Meg cuts a hole in the box, but Jason says that's not the right type of window and explains that it can't just be a square: it's like four small windows all in one. Meg tears that wall down and tries again. By lunch Jason has decided the rooms need doors, not just openings, but because the windows were wrong, he wants to draw the doors before they get messed up too. They also need something other than pens to draw with.

"Houses have colors," he says.

When Meg crawls out of the dark interior of the construction she realizes they haven't been building a fort. It *is* a house. She can see it coming together, lopsided but recognizable.

"Mother!" she calls. "Where are the markers?"

The doorbell rings and it's the man from the electric company. Although their mother has already had the same conversation with the employee on the phone yesterday, she prods the man on the porch for better answers as to why the electric wasn't hooked up on time.

"We need markers," Jason whines.

Their mother gives Meg another twenty dollars and tells them to go buy more at CVS.

Meg is somewhat annoyed that the fort-house building is actually entertaining. She knows she's too old for stuff like this. A few months ago, she even swore off cartoons because they were childish—but that lasted all of a few weeks. Her mother had said one morning, before they moved, when Meg refused to watch TV—demanding instead to be taken to the library—that Meg was trying to grow up too quickly. The night before that Meg had watched a nature special on PBS and learned that banana slugs could change their biological sex. She'd wanted a book on the mating habits of slugs, but her mother said, *I can't have this talk right now*, even though Meg was not interested in people sex.

Meg was eleven, almost twelve. Now her mother was no longer complaining about Meg's hurry to grow up. She seemed instead to assume it had just happened, overnight, and that Meg wasn't a kid anymore. Meg herself wasn't sure if she was or wasn't. She didn't need a bedtime and she could do homework without help and she needed a training bra, but there were still times when she wanted to cry and still times when she didn't know answers to adult questions and she still felt emotions she didn't understand at all. When their mother put Jason in counseling, she asked Meg if she wanted to go too. When Meg didn't have an answer right away her mother had taken it as a no and said, *You're handling this so well. I'm so proud of you.*

Jason is humming the song *Head, Shoulders, Knees and Toes.*

"What are we building anyway?" Meg asks. "Is it a fort or a house?"

"It's a house."

"What kind of house? A mansion? A cottage?"

"This isn't the way," Jason says beneath the stop sign, looking farther down the street where they'd walked yesterday.

"I know, but if we go this way we walk by Charlie's house."

"I don't want to go that way. It'll take too long."

"What's the hurry? The fort-house will still be there." Meg is crossing the road already.

"I don't want to go that way!" Jason yells.

"Shut up!" Meg has a premonition of walking in front of Charlie's house with Jason behind her screaming his face red, Charlie hearing it, and looking out the window and seeing Meg struggle with her little brother. "C'mon. I'll buy you a Coke." Their mother won't let Jason have soft drinks. She says he's too young for them.

Jason looks down the street as if he's going to argue or walk on without her, but then he steps into the road and joins her.

"It's a house in a house," he tells her.

"A house in a house?"

"A house that isn't haunted."

Meg isn't sure if he means the house they live in or the one they're building.

"And no ghosts can get in because no one was murdered in it," Jason adds.

Meg can see Charlie's house at the corner. It is big and yellow with white trim. She imagines Charlie inside. She imagines he's reading *The Golden Compass* too. She imagines that's why her own mother had to buy her copy instead of getting it from the library: Charlie had the only copy checked out. Since it's summer vacation and Charlie has nothing better to do, he's also gotten out his yearbook and when he's tired of reading he looks through the pictures of the girls and tries to decide who he'll ask out next year. Because Meg's picture is located on the top right of a page, he sees it every time he flips through. He looks at her freckles and thinks they're pretty. He notes how mature her dress is; no more bows and lace for her. When they run into him in CVS he'll say, *Hey*, and she'll act cool, like she's real grown up because she's a babysitter now too, and she'll ask him what he's reading and he'll say *The Golden Compass* and then she'll ask him if he's seen the movie and did he want to ever come over and watch it and he'd say yes.

"...but a house has to have stuff in it too. No one lives in an empty house," Jason is saying.

"Uh huh. We can put some blankets and lamps in it."

"No it needs to be *real* stuff."

"That *is* real stuff."

Meg slows her walk as they get to Charlie's house. She came to his birthday party last year. In Charlie's backyard he'd told her that he was scared about high school. *Everything is going to change*, he said, and he seemed sad about it. Meg had tried to cheer him up and she'd lied and said she knew all about high school. She'd read lots of books on it, and that it wasn't very different at all. Charlie had smiled and said, *yeah, maybe*, while stripping bark off a tree. Later she thought about how eventually they'd carve their initials into that tree in the shape of a heart the way people do in movies.

But today there is no Charlie. No one outside. No one at the window waiting for her to walk by.

"Jason," she says, stopping in the middle of the sidewalk.

"Told you this would take too long. I didn't want to come this way."

Charlie's house looks remarkably like the house being built in their living room. There are differences of course; their house is not painted and is not two stories. But the windows are the same, down to the ratio of their height to the walls of the house, and their house has the same jutted kitchen and living room and even the eave above the front door is the same.

*

When they return with markers and pencils and gummy bears— Meg having already disposed of Jason's empty Coke can in a neighbor's trash bin—their mother is hanging pictures. The wall under the stairs is an eclectic assortment of frames and photos: family memories.

As Meg looks at the wall and then at her mother on the stepstool, nails in her mouth, frame under arm, her wedding ring shining, she realizes that her father will never be gone. She knows this thought should comfort her; it's the type of thing Jason's therapist might say— *You'll never really be alone; when you think about him he'll always be with you.* But it's not the right kind of "he'll never be gone."

Now that the photos are going up, Meg looks around and sees her father everywhere. He's sitting on the sofa next to the fort-house drinking coffee and reading the paper; he's in the kitchen, scouring the cast-iron frying pan that rarely leaves the stove top. He's in the entry way, hanging his long, black coat on the hall tree. The coffee table under which he always left his work shoes. The kitchen table with the loose leg he always complained about but never fixed. The gold-rimmed bowl where he would leave his keys. The house has changed but the things in it have not. Even the things outside the house are the same: oak trees in the yard, her father lying under one, her mother beside him screaming, Jason in the tree crying, an ambulance coming.

*

Jason scrawls on scrap pieces of cardboard, showing Meg what the door should look like, the crown molding, the wood paneling in the kitchen. Jason draws the outlines, Meg the details. They are almost done with the kitchen when their mother tells them to wash up for Chinese food.

"Well look at this," she says. There are flecks of paint and drywall in her hair. "Look at what you guys have done."

"It's not finished yet." Jason is inside the fort-house with a red marker. He is coloring the cabinets. He looks at his mother through the cut-out window and grins.

"We need more markers." Meg holds up the brown Crayola; she's worn the soft nub down and she shakes it. "All out."

"If you guys are going to color the whole thing we might as well buy paint. You know we're going to have to move this right? I need to put down the rug."

"You can't take it down," Jason says.

"I'm not going to take it down, we'll just have to pick it up and roll the rug under it." She tells Meg to listen for the doorbell while she takes a shower.

Meg is coloring the window boxes outside the kitchen. "I don't think she was serious about paint. We're going to have to color this. You think yellow? If we do yellow it's going to look like puke." She's already tested the yellow marker on the cardboard; it isn't strong or vibrant enough to cover the brown.

"I don't know yet. Stop bothering me." Jason is wrinkling his nose, his face very close to the cardboard wall, inspecting the outlines still yet to be filled.

When the delivery man comes and tells Meg the total is $23.46, she does the math with a green marker on cardboard and signs for their dinner. She leaves it on the floor and asks Jason for the red marker. She needs to color the tulips.

It's difficult to coax Jason out of the fort-house. While his mother unrolls the rug—a Persian monstrosity that has been leaning, bent in half against the wall—Jason hops from foot to foot like he has to pee, running between their mother and Meg as one pushes the carpet and one maneuvers the fort-house. He bends at the waist, the knees, turning his head, rubbing his forehead like he's thinking very hard, all the while saying, *careful, careful*, as if his art may get damaged.

Then he almost falls asleep at the dinner table. The sun has set, and Meg hardly noticed. The lights are working. The house is flooded with them.

"Thank you for helping your brother," her mother says, picking up their plates and scraping remnant noodles and carrots into the sink. Meg's fingers ache and her hands cramp, but building the fort-house has been good. It has made her *not* think.

After their mother carries Jason upstairs, Meg sits on her bed and looks around her room. The dresser on the far wall was a weekend project: her mother found it at an antique store and Meg and her dad had sanded it down and painted it robin's egg blue. It was the only weekend she could remember where it was just her and him.

She tries to read but she's tired of thinking about the labor of helping others, how the children in her book are responsible for so much. She closes it and looks at the door. She can almost see her father in the dark checking in on her, the way he used to do when he thought she was sleeping.

*

Meg wakes in the night. She's been dreaming about her father and in the dream, he is a bird—a robin, an eagle, a crow—and he's trying to tell her something but it all sounds like squawks to her.

She tosses her blanket off and leaves her room. Jason is sleeping in his bed and sucking his thumb. Downstairs she looks into the kitchen and sees the table where every morning her father would tell the same joke—*What do you want to eat, rhinoceros toenails?*—pouring cereal into their bowls and lamenting the terrible things his children wanted for breakfast.

She turns and enters the living room, crawls through the front door of the house-fort. With the lights off, she realizes that the moon is shining through the faux windows, through the faux door. In the living room the flower print couch is pushed up against the wall. The ottoman's leather fabric gleams. They are oddly shaped, imprecise, and the colors seem to seep out of their boundaries, as if the furniture is fuzzy, as if Meg is looking at it all through squinted eyes. The cardboard feels warm under her hands and feet and she slides her limbs along the faux floor, lays down on the sofa, and goes to sleep.

*

Jason was pretending to be a cat. He was on all fours and crawling around saying *me-ow, me-ow.*

It's meow, Meg told him. *Not me ow.*

Jason sidled up next to her, bumped her so hard she dropped her book.

Stop it. Go be a cat somewhere else.

Jason went into the front yard and was a cat out there. He tried to sneak up on some birds but they flew away. He practiced his *meow* and sharpened his claws against the tree. And then he climbed the tree because that's what cats do. Cats also get stuck in trees, and Jason did that too.

Meg heard the garage door open, but it didn't close. When she looked outside, she saw her father crossing the lawn in his suit and tie, holding the ladder.

Dad's doing yard work in his dress clothes, she yelled.

Meg and her mother went out the front door. Meg's father was setting the ladder up against the tree. Jason was in the branches and was hiccupping. *Get me down, Dad.*

How long has he been up there? Their mother still had a dish towel in her hands.

Meg's father was at the top of the ladder. The ladder was rocking. His arms were flapping. He was at the base of the tree, motionless.

*

Charlie's mother had come to collect Meg and Jason while their mother went in the ambulance with their father. Meg didn't even know her mother and Charlie's mother were friends.

Charlie was standing in the doorway of his kitchen when they arrived at the house. Meg and Jason were told to sit at the table and cups of cocoa were put in front of them even though it was April outside and too hot for warm drinks. Jason had stopped crying, but he kept saying, "It's my fault. I was pretending to be a cat."

The phone rang and Charlie picked it up, carrying the receiver into the hallway where Meg couldn't see him. "Mom," he said, reappearing, nodding as if some secret was shared between them, and she took the phone from him.

"I'm really sorry about your dad. I hope he's okay." Charlie came to the table but didn't sit down. His hands were shoved in his pockets and he looked at the floor.

"Yeah." Meg didn't look at him either.

"You want to like, do something, to keep your mind off it?"

"No. I don't know. No. I want to wait here."

"Okay."

Charlie's mother had also gone into the hallway. Meg could hear her talking but couldn't make out what she was saying. It was like she was whispering into the wall.

"Jason, you want to play some video games? I got *Donkey Kong*."

Meg and Jason weren't allowed to have video games. Jason slid off his chair and followed Charlie, returning to get his coffee cup of cocoa.

When Charlie's mother hung up the phone, she took Jason's seat but didn't say anything.

"Meg," Jason called. "Come play."

Meg couldn't get up. She didn't want to look at Jason. She didn't want to play games. She wanted her mother, and her father, but all she had was Charlie's mother who clearly didn't know what to do.

*

Meg wakes up in the fort-house. Her neck hurts. The sofa pillow she was using is gone. So is the sofa and the ottoman. A blanket is twisted around her legs and her mouth tastes sour. She runs into her mother on the stairs.

"Did you sleep down here?" She looks at the blanket in Meg's hands.

"Yeah. Couldn't go to sleep. Came down to read," she lies.

"I guess now at least Jason stays put."

After breakfast their mother rearranges furniture and unpacks boxes. The washer and dryer hum from the laundry room next to the kitchen. She keeps disappearing into the back room where all their father's office boxes are. She keeps turning the radio on then off. Finally she just turns the TV on and asks Meg and Jason what they want to watch, but they say they don't care. They need to finish the fort-house.

"Wouldn't it be cool if we brought a table in here? Or like, some chairs or pillows?" Meg is sitting on the sofa, surveying their work. The green, red, brown, and blue markers have gone dry too. Jason is inside coloring in the kitchen counters; they're black.

"No. We don't need anything. Everything we need is right here. Look at all this stuff." They've drawn furniture and pictures on the walls but neither has been trained for art and there is no perspective. The rooms are flat.

"We could get a mini-fridge!"

"No. We have a fridge. We don't need two fridges," Jason says.

"Jason, let's go." Their mother has her purse and car keys. It is time for Jason's psychologist appointment.

*

While they are gone, Meg decides that the shingles need to be colored. She goes into the back room to pick through the boxes in case there are some forgotten markers. The furniture is pushed against the wall. She remembers her father standing in front of his desk and playing tickle monster; the goal was to run past him and sit in the ergonomic chair to claim the throne, but he always caught up Meg and Jason and dug his fingers into their armpits and stomachs. When she remembers this, she flees the room.

When Jason and her mother return a few hours later, they have not bought markers and their mother is telling Jason that she's glad he likes Dr. Hoffman. *She* likes Dr. Wallis. It's good that they like their doctors. When Meg reminds her about the depleting markers, their mother gives her another twenty dollars and tells her to get as many packages of markers as she can.

On the way to CVS, Meg takes the long route. Jason does not complain. His fingers are color-stained and he holds his hands out to the side, snagging leaves off bushes and shrubs.

"Mom says you've been getting in her bed at night," Meg says.

"No I haven't."

"Not the past couple of nights, but before that, yeah."

"I had nightmares," Jason admits.

"And now you don't?" In front of them a black cat is slinking across a lawn. Meg wants to tell Jason about how black cats are bad luck, but she doesn't. "Not even in a haunted house?"

"I don't think our house is haunted. You said we only have to get worried if ghosts were murdered."

"Did you tell your doctor about the boy who died in our house?" Meg imagines an array of possible outcomes from this: her mother's disappointment, grounding, maybe she'll be sent to a doctor too.

Jason remains quiet.

"You swore on Floppy Ears, remember?"

"Yeah, but, he's gone. Anyway, you don't have to worry. The house isn't haunted." He nods his head as if assuring himself.

Meg wonders what happened in the therapist's office, what Jason's doctor said to him to coax out the story, what the doctor said to him to make everything alright, to make Jason so unafraid, so certain he shouldn't be concerned or worried. It seems unfair that he gets all the answers.

Ahead of them a woman is standing in Charlie's lawn. She is struggling with a sign, her high heels sinking in the grass as she tries to shimmy it into the earth. It is not Charlie's mother.

"What are you doing?" Meg sounds more accusatory than she means to while pointing at the sign.

The woman looks up, her hands still working. "Putting a for-sale sign in the yard. You interested?" Something in the way the woman responds is as equally accusatory. The way she suggests Meg might want to buy it, the way it is clear Meg is just a kid and doesn't have the money to. The woman laughs when Meg doesn't say anything. Meg doesn't know if it's because what the woman said is ridiculous or because Meg's face makes it clear she is upset: her eyebrows have gone up, her lips turn down.

Meg can see now through the windows that the house is empty: no curtains, no furniture, no lights, no Charlie. "But he didn't even say goodbye."

"Kid, your whole life is going to be full of no goodbyes. This is good practice."

Meg reaches for Jason's hand, pulls him along and sticks her tongue out at the woman. "Bitch."

*

She hurries Jason through CVS and back to the house. At home, Meg begins constructing tables and cups out of cardboard, but when she tries to bring them into the fort-house Jason yells at her and from upstairs Meg hears her mother yell at her too.

"Don't you get it?" she asks her brother. "It's not a house without *stuff.*"

"It does have *stuff.*" Jason looks around at all their drawings on the cardboard wall. "You just want *stupid stuff.*"

"I'm done with this fort," Meg says, tossing the cup she's made across the room. It isn't a very good cup. The cardboard is stiff and won't roll smoothly. The cup is all angles.

"It's not a *fort.* It's a *house.*"

Meg reads in the backyard instead. She holds the book up so that she can't see the oak tree, but she keeps lowering it too, looking at the grass at the base of the tree, her father there, not there. She's almost done with the novel. She reads until the porch light comes on and her mother says it's time for dinner and then she reads through dinner while her mother and brother talk about a coloring book Jason has just remembered. There used to be a whole series of coloring books that needed only water. A cheap brush dipped in water, when applied to the page, produced color with no paint. Meg knew the pages were treated with something that made the color appear, but she also remembered how fun it was to paint this way, to not know what something was going to look like, to have no control over the end product and despite that, to like it.

"But I don't need those now," Jason says. "I can help with the dishes."

"Jason," their mother says, "how nice of you."

*

Meg wakes that night and thinks she hears her father. She wanders downstairs into the living room where his voice tells her to make sure her homework is done. The space between the sofa and chest of drawers is empty. This used to be where she would sit on her father's foot and he would hold up his leg while he tried to shake her off. She can hear him laughing from inside the fort-house but when she crawls in, he's not there either. She lays down on the sofa and stares out the window.

*

When she wakes for the second time that night, she *knows* her father is in the fort-house. He is closing the bathroom door. He is humming in the kitchen. He is pouring coffee.

"Dad?"

Meg gets up from the sofa and crawls into the next room.

"Dad?"

"Right here, ladybug."

"Dad, where are you?" Meg crawls from room to room. He is not in the bathroom. He is not on the back porch. He is not in the dining room. She knows the song he's singing, *Head, Shoulder, Knees, and Toes,* but every time she turns a cardboard corner the voice seems to come from someplace else.

"Dad, I can hear you but can't see you. Where are you?"

"Just through here, ladybug."

Meg has arrived back in the living room. The furniture seems crowded by the low ceiling. The fan is on and the chain hanging from it makes a faint clinking noise. Inside Charlie's mother's display cabinet the good china has fallen over. The video game boxes next the TV are all open. There is a glass on the coffee table half full of orange juice. The lamp shaped like a horse is on and is lighting a door in the wall. It is a door Meg did not put there, and it is a door Jason did not draw. It is just high enough for her to crawl through.

"In here, ladybug," her father says.

Meg's hand reaches for the knob. It is dark metal and cold. It is oval-shaped and hard to turn. When she pushes, she feels her knees slide off the soft cardboard. She is in a dark room. She can stand, and in the moonlight coming through the window she sees the clock on the mantle that her father gave to her mother last Christmas—when he looked at it he always made the same joke: *A freckle past a hair.*

The floorboards above her creek. Then Jason is behind her, his small hand on her lower back. "What are you doing?"

AN ORACLE

Every generation a new Oracle is chosen: she is always a girl of twelve, the choosing always occurs the day after the old Oracle dies, and the new Oracle is always chosen by a cow. If I didn't live on this island, didn't grow up with gaseous caves and earthquakes and hadn't been prepared for this possibility since I was five, I might laugh at the part about the cow. But I am twelve, and do live here, and this morning I wake up to find the Namer of Oracles outside my window, her wide black nose smearing snot and water on the glass, her garland of flowers broken and half-eaten and somehow still draped around her neck.

I sit back on my bed and stare at her. I want to hate the cow, but she's just as much a victim of circumstance as I am now. People come from all around the world to ask the Oracle questions. They are almost always unhappy when they leave. What they don't understand is that an Oracle has no control over what she utters, doesn't usually remember any of it, and cannot decipher the cryptic messages that issue forth from her own mouth. We do not choose this life, a cow chooses it for us, and we're all just dolls for the gods to arrange how they choose. No girl in her right mind would choose to age quickly, sit in a cave on a fault line, inhale noxious sulfurous fumes, fall into seizures, be hope and hate together in a hideous marbling. At least for the next two months I will slowly be trained, not thrown into the brokenness like a piece of steak to the dogs. As I look at the cow, all I can think about is how she will be the one butchered.

I am awake before my parents, but already our neighbors are emerging from their white-washed houses, standing on gravel paths or in the rocky meadow, looking at the Namer of Oracles. I can see them out the window, awkward statues. I can see Kristina too, paler than the rest, skin so white her veins look like lapis. I get up, put on a robe, and go outside. The cow is waiting for me, her head a furry triangle, and I take her lead and begin the descent down the hillside. No one follows me. It's against the rules. I am supposed to lead the cow to the police station where she lives in an open barn and then the mayor will record my name in a book made of real parchment: the skin of former Namers. Then I will go home and eat breakfast. Collect what I want to take with me to my new life. Move up into the hills where I will live next to the cave where I will sit and make predictions as the Oracle.

But right now, it doesn't feel any different. I suppose the few times I considered the possibility of being named Oracle I thought it might be something akin to being a superhero. We're told there will be changes, but none of us like to think the grim life they outline will be the truth. As I walk, the cow's bell clangs behind me, the ground feels the same, I have no superhuman strength, the compost piles don't smell any sweeter, and I am twelve and still have no boobs. I pray it takes longer than normal for me to transform.

The cow halts every so often and I cannot budge her. She is eating grass or weeds or sometimes she just stares and moos at nothing. A walk that should take ten minutes takes thirty and by the time I make it to the police station the mayor is waiting outside for me in a purple pinstripe suit with a matching bowler hat. I'm sure he got a call right away and got up with enough time to put on his finery. The police chief is there with a camera and he's taking pictures of me and the cow as we approach and I wish I had put on real clothes and not just this robe. The mayor shakes my hand and together we lead the cow into the barn. I realize I do not know her name, and I whisper into her velvet ear "Who are you?" before the mayor claims me, writes my name with a grand flourish near the front steps, and sends me on my way. When I return my parents are awake and excited but I go in my room and lock the door. I no longer have a name. I am *the Oracle* and I want to pull an Ino and jump off a cliff, escaping the madness I know my life is about to become.

*

The old Oracle was a nice woman as far as I can tell. A little loopy, but I'm told she was always like that, even before. I find out by reading the paper my dad shoves under my door that she choked on an almond and asphyxiated. People knew to go check on her when the Namer of Oracles just wandered off in the morning to choose the new Oracle, and it just so happened that she was dressed for the occasion. She's kind of a celebrity. Townspeople bring her snacks and magazines to look at, though she usually just eats the paper, and we dress her up in scarves, and if someone takes the time, occasionally she'll get a flower garland. Some of the dwarf iris blooms are still on the ground outside my window. They are wilted and flat in the sun.

I wish the old Oracle hadn't died so prematurely—she was only fifty-two—because then I could stay in school and go to university and become a financial analyst. I am not sure exactly what this means but Constantine Polodorius did this and now when he returns to the island to visit he comes on a yacht and brings the entire town tins of Turkish Delight, disgusting powder-coated candies that none of us like but that we eat anyway because it is exotic.

I am recalling the name of his boat, the Heliotrope, and biting my nails down to the quick when I realize the changes are already beginning to occur.

"Sweetie," my mom says, scratching at my door, "do you want breakfast?"

I do not answer and I can see the shadows of her slippered feet begin to move away, come back, and then leave again. Instead of bleeding I am oozing nectar. I am careful not to chew on my fingers anymore. It's too much like self-cannibalism.

My father is talking with neighbors. I can hear them laughing and they're probably congratulating him on his Oracle daughter. I want to run to him and for him to save me, but my father is no longer my father, my mother no longer my mother. I know this in my bones the way I know I was their daughter yesterday. They are beginning to feel distant and I begin to feel lightheaded. I think a seizure may be coming on.

*

My new house is built into a cliff side. It has a thatch roof and blue sod is planted on top of it. Because I am the Oracle I never have to cook. My meals are provided by villagers and people who travel to see me so I do not have an entire kitchen, which means my friends and I sit at a tacky Formica table in the one room that is my home as the keepers turn tourists away, explaining that the Oracle cannot see anyone for two months. There are shouts about travel costs and polytheistic heresy.

"So, this is it?" Kristina asks, looking around. People say we could have been sisters, and a few people say we are. My mother had twins but the rule is the rule and the weaker one is always exposed. When I was five, Kristina wandered into town. We have the same brown eyes and our brown hair waves in the same places. She usually wears hers up so people can tell us apart but today it's down around her shoulders in an act of solidarity.

"It's not…bad." Vicky is trying to be optimistic, but I just slam my forehead back onto the tabletop. "No, really," she assures me. "We could paint the walls and get some posters and you're the Oracle so you could totally demand movie channels…" Her statement dies down as she looks at my TV. It is not a flat screen and it has rabbit ears. "You could get a new TV," she says quietly.

"You guys, this is going to suck." I look at them, Kristina with her eyes like fissures erupting and Vicky, splotchy and blushing to her blonde roots with embarrassment. "Maybe you can still bring me homework assignments and stuff. Keep me in the loop with classes."

"You still want to do homework?" Vicky asks, astonished.

"I gotta do something," I mumble.

"There's a great view of the sea," Kristina says, pushing back her chair along the hardwood floor. "You're close enough to see the dolphins. Maybe you could take up landscape painting."

There is a knock at the door. I get up, but decide to ignore it. I go to stand beside Kristina and I hold her hand. It feels like my hand, the same moist palms, nails manicured to the same length.

"Should I get it?" Vicky squeaks.

Kristina and I are breathing in the same rhythm. "When will you come back?" I ask.

"Soon."

The keepers are here for my instruction. They tell me it is time for my friends to leave, reminding me I can only have visitors once a week, and then they ask if there is anything I require. As Kristina and Vicky dejectedly wave goodbye, I demand, in my most regal voice, to have the cow brought to me.

*

There are rules about being an Oracle. An Oracle can only accept visitors on Mondays, an Oracle is a woman at twelve, an Oracle may not wear revealing clothing and must remain a virgin, which sucks, and an Oracle must devote her life to the mysteries, which means no school, no vacation. An Oracle cannot be vain and an Oracle cannot have mirrors in her home. There are no rules about whether or not an Oracle can have a pet so the keepers have to bring me the cow, even though they protest against it and try to plead tradition.

"The cow lives at the police station," they whine in unison, a chorus of mindless, bald men.

"The cow now lives with me," I tell them. "For the next week."

In a week from today, there will be a feast in my honor and the cow will be slaughtered for offerings and barbeque and then a new cow will be chosen when the smoke from the fire moves with the wind and chooses one of the other town cows that will be all lined up, ten feet apart from each other, in a line as long as it needs to be. That damn cow deserves more than that, I think, and I tell the keepers as much.

Within a few hours there are craftsmen at my house building a shelter for the cow and I am reading Heraclitus and his ridiculous account of the Pythia's prediction to Croesus and I am reminded that people are going to hear what they want, see what they want, no matter what I say. I could fall into a trance and tell someone that they are in for a great and wonderful surprise and they'd ignore the promotion they get and claim that the free bible handed out in front of the nudie bar is a sign that they are meant to be Christian. The one thing I can't say is that I'm not the Oracle.

I have decided to name the cow Ariadne. It may not follow myth, but they're both being treated in a metaphorically similar sense, so whatever. Ariadne seems oblivious to the workmen who are hastily putting up rough beams, whole trees really, only cleared of their branches and turned upside down so the roots don't take to the earth. She is content to swing her tail to shoo the flies away and to watch men doing all the hard work.

"Okay then," I say to her, resting my elbow on her back. "What do you think?"

She does not answer but I did not expect her to. The area is quiet except for the pounding of hammers and nails since the keepers have blocked the path up to the caves. One workman who I don't recognize is especially cute, and I wonder what happens if I don't remain a virgin. Not that I'd get a chance to test it.

*

My cottage is next to the caves, which I have yet to explore. "Not too much too fast," the keepers tell me. Bullshit. When they're gone tonight, I'm taking Ariadne and a flashlight and going in anyway. It seems strange now that I've never been up here before. It's beautiful in its own desolate way, and already it's beginning to feel like home. I don't know if this is because I need it to be, or if it is because of the changes. Regardless, the view of the island from up here reveals it to be sparse and rocky; there is a reason why our people are traditionally herdsmen and not farmers. There are few trees, and the ones that grow are either tall, slender pines or squat, bushy olive trees. I'm told these grow more readily on the west side of the island where the ruined castle complex is, another place I've never been. It's over the mountains, not far, but seemingly impossible to pass when you're a teenager without a car.

This new home is about two kilometers up a wide dirt path that has been carved out of the hills. The east side of it has been fortified with flat white stones, a low wall to keep rocks and landslides from tumbling into the way of tourists. This path ends near the entrance to the cave, which used to be just a hole in the schist, a granite-like rock found only here. Now they've built a permanent wooden door shoved into a circular frame and above it, carved into the rock, is a bull's head with gilded horns.

Oracles used to be associated with a certain god or goddess, but we've abandoned that now. We don't know who speaks through us, only that this island is its own entity and that like our ancient ancestors, we fear earthquakes that can ruin us and the thundering tread of invisible bulls hammering the earth apart with their hooves. I seem to remember the sounds of stone falling, the curved feel of a cold bathtub, the heat of flame, as some other Oracle's home fell to the centuries. I wonder why we don't use a bull to choose the new Oracle. Perhaps the keepers are worried about a young girl getting gored.

*

When I wake it is dark, wolves are howling, and the cow's bell is fervent. I step outside and see Ariadne with her hooves against the wall of the house, reaching her thick neck to my roof, trying to get at the blue grass. She looks absurd and awkward, so I give her a gentle push. She moves to the side with an angry moo and I stand on a rock and gather tufts of grass in my fists to throw down to the ground for her. My bones are creaking and I fear I'm aging too fast. Even the effort of feeding the cow has left me winded and sore and my stomach is cramping. I go inside to find a flashlight and when I do, I switch it on to see the sun-bleached hair on my arms and legs as dark lines; my down has become pin feathers.

Outside I grab Ariadne's rope harder than I mean to, but she is not put off. She's eaten all the grass and trails behind me to the cave entrance where I pull the door open and peek inside. Our people used to believe that one of the entrances to the underworld was here, in this cave system. I can almost believe it. The rock moans and shifts in the cooler night air and somewhere below, Sisyphus is rolling his boulder up an incline. White cloth has been rigged up around the walls. The cave smells like rotting eggs and is not impressive. We cross the first room, Ariadne's bell echoing, and I pull the curtains back to reveal the Oracle's chamber. It's a closet with a door at the back. On the ground is a brazier and a thick blue cushion. This is my cubicle. Ariadne pushes in and steps on my eventual seat, leaving a dirty mark on the cushion, and I try the door but it is locked. Behind it are more tunnels, I know, but how many and how deep I can only guess.

*

The keepers demand that I coat my body in olive oil, exercise, then scrape it off with a strigil, a scythe-shaped grooming device that will clean my skin and shave my newly darkened hair. I ask them why I can't have a razor and they chime together, "tradition, tradition," and I know I've already pushed my luck with the cow.

I pour oil from a flask into my palm. I am sure this is going to make me break out. Afterwards, I go outside in my swimsuit, for posterity's sake, and jog up and down the path until I feel like I can no longer breathe. In the privacy of my cottage I scrape of the top layer of skin, see the hairs come away. I still want to take a shower and when I do, I notice blood pooling near the drain. I have not cut myself; I am becoming a woman, and I am relieved to know that not all of my insides are thick and golden.

*

I read that the ancient Oracles were epileptic. That they were chosen because of this. Now it seems as though seizures simply come with the job. I'm relatively sure I've only had two seizures so far. One on my first day, and the other yesterday, Wednesday, because I blacked out and woke up on the living room floor. The keepers assure me that in time I'll only have them when I'm making predictions. This does not comfort me.

What does comfort me is Ariadne. I have been taking my books outside and reading aloud to her, but now I've managed to shove her through my doorway and she stands in my cottage with her head out the window towards the sea. She moos from time to time, long bellowing sounds that make me laugh. She is fawn-colored and warm and prefers sour apples to sweet and she knows not to shit indoors.

I am carving her portrait right now into a banana peel with a toothpick. When I look up, her head is missing, exposed to the breeze through the window. Tomorrow the lines I've etched will be dark and creased and I wonder if there is some sealant I can use to preserve this memento of us. When I am done, I stand beside her and reach out the window to scratch the top of her head. She is mooing at the dolphins down below and her pink tongue is testing the salt air.

*

Today is a trial run. Ariadne tries to follow me into the cave, but the keepers shut her out. I am made to sit on the cushion in the closet and am instructed to burn some herbs in the brazier. I complain that it's hot in the closet and the keepers ask, "What is a closet?"

While I am waiting for a seizure to kick in, I quietly stand and try the mystery door again. It won't budge, but upon further inspection, does not have a lock either.

Apparently, when asked by a keeper about the state of the country's fiscal cliff, I predict that *with great gain comes great sacrifice.* They take this to mean that there *will* be a financial recovery and I take it to mean that they are incapable of interpreting predictions correctly. When I emerge from behind the curtain they are bobbing their heads like baby birds and I plead exhaustion. I walk back to the cottage and more time has passed than I thought. It is almost night and I realize that the seizures will put me out for hours. It only felt like minutes. How much of my life's time will be spent in limbo now?

When the keepers have retreated down the path, I push Ariadne into the cottage and I give her a bucket of water with crushed lemons, which she knocks over while moving her bulk around the small space. She moos at the window. I open it and she thrusts her head out. The skin on my hands looks thinner and more stretched, my fingers slender with swollen knuckles. I do not have a mirror and cannot see what I am becoming. I am beginning to understand the rules.

The twin bed is across the room and I push it towards the window. I leave enough room for Ariadne to stand and then I lay down. She smells a little sour, and like hay, but she is alive and breathing and her gentle snorts make me feel less alone.

*

I wake up to the sound of askomandouras being carried up from the village. The festivities and music have started. Ariadne is standing at the door, waiting to be let outside. I expose us both to morning sun and find a tray of spanakopita and a basket of fruit. I wish someone would bring me a hamburger.

Kristina is coming up the path towards me. She is wearing a long yellow dress with an empire waist and she looks like a goddess. I count the days in my head. Today is visitor's day. And today, Ariadne will go to be with the gods.

Kristina and I sit on rock and eat and Ariadne walks in circles. Perhaps she knows her time is up. She seems antsy.

I ask Kristina how I look.

"Different," she says, without apology.

We compare arms and yes, I can see that my skin looks older and lacks a certain shine. Liver spots are starting to appear.

"It's supposed to be this way," she says, and then quieter, "if I could trade places with you I would."

When Kristina came to the village no one wanted to take her in. Finally old Yia Yia did, but the woman doesn't care much for Kristina. Kristina's family is a river and oranges and being the Oracle would be fitting for her. She has always been alone and unwelcomed and she bears it well. If she was the Oracle, at least sometimes, she might feel needed.

When I was younger, I tried to get my parents to take her in. My father pleaded Oedipus and told me that the Oracle had made a prediction to him: *your first child will be a great joy, your second a great shame*. We did not know if Kristina was the exposed daughter who was supposed to die. My father wouldn't take the chance that she was. It seems the prophecy has come true, assuming Kristina *is* my sister, and assuming we weren't mixed up after birth and I'm really the second born. I've never told her about the prophecy and never will.

"Tell me it sucks down there," I say, referring to the village. "Tell me it's boring and stupid and that I'm much better up here."

"It's boring and stupid and you're much better up here," she says, and then we both laugh.

We play four games of backgammon and I lose every time.

"How come Vicky didn't come?" I ask. "Or my parents?"

"I don't think it's the same for them anymore," she admits, and she is right. I know *I* care less about them, and assume they feel the same way. It upsets me that I'm losing my own history. I am still managing to love Kristina, though, even if there is a veil between us. "They don't view you as *you* anymore. You're the Oracle," she continues.

"How do you see me?"

"You're a girl and my best friend and the only person I love and until you tell me to leave I'll be here."

I cry and put my head in her lap. She stokes my hair which is beginning to fall out in grey strands, and she tells me a story about a princess who sleeps under a spell for a hundred years.

*

They've lit the path down to the village with oil-filled torches. Below, the people are waiting for me to appear with Ariadne. I have dressed her in eleven garlands and she is trying to eat all of them.

We stand near the cave and I am apologizing to her. "I won't eat you, I promise," I tell her.

The instruments are playing, and I know the procession is eager to start. I've forced the keepers to retreat to the rest of the people. I have been given a white dress and a wig. I am wearing neither. Instead I have on denim shorts and a tank top. I am not going to the festival.

I click on the flashlight and pull Ariadne towards the cave. Inside, she waits while I try the closet door again. When it still doesn't open, I kick it until the old wood splinters and I am weak with effort. It finally jars loose, a century of dust floating in the air around us. Behind it is a tunnel and Ariadne almost pushes me over to get into it.

We fit side by side and walk for a long time. The ground begins to slope downwards and the sulfur smell increases. It is cool and windy; the tunnel must have other openings, but we do not see any.

Legend has it that these tunnels were once part of the island's castle complex. The castle was abandoned thousands of years ago. Archeologists say its destruction was due to the earthquakes. They actually discovered *three* castle complexes buried under rock and dirt. It fell three times before my ancestors gave up. Before their gods abandoned them and drove them into the ocean in boats that took them to the mainland.

I do not know how these caves and tunnels can be attached to that broken down and forgotten place. It's on the other side of the island with the olive groves and this tunnel would have to run for almost 200 kilometers.

I wonder when they'll come looking for me.

When we reach a river, I estimate that we have been walking for close to two hours. It is a bad estimate because it could be four or one. I don't have a watch. Ariadne is doing well but I am tired and my old bones ache. I should be surprised that water is here, but I am not. Something else has come with being the Oracle, an intuition that tells me my two-thousand-year life is remembered in this leathered skin. When we come to the river I am excited for the first time in a week. It is small, maybe a creek, if a person can define a creek by being in a cave. On the other side, the tunnel opens into a cavern so large my flashlight cannot find the walls. On the other side, there is a tree, a pomegranate tree, and I am hungry.

We step into the black water and I think we both hear the voices. Ariadne's ears twitch but she doesn't stop. I don't even have to hold her rope anymore. I wonder where we'll be put. The fields of punishment for abandoning my post. The Asphodel Meadows for ordinary, indifferent folk. The Elysian Fields, for heroes. I am not sure what I am anymore.

When the keepers discover us gone, I do not know what will happen. There will be no smoke from Ariadne's fire to choose a new cow. Without a new cow there can be no new Oracle. Without an Oracle... I'm not sure what happens. I imagine Kristina laughing at them all, calling them fools and then running into the night to live our life. Maybe we're both the second child. Prophecies are strange like that. The Oracle never said the first child had to survive. Perhaps that child died as a cluster of cells in my mother's uterus and none of us are any the wiser.

Someone is calling us home. I pluck a fruit from the tree and rend it in half, holding one part of it out. Ariadne crunches through the skin and the juice explodes across her fur, a battle wound for the words she never had. The other half, I eat seed by seed, letting each burst in my mouth, coating my teeth in tart red juice that tastes like home.

SEA ROOM

I have just turned nineteen and Daniel Sanders has died; upon his passing, Ms. Kennedy discovered a wooden ship, half-submerged, in a pond on the old man's property just south of where we argue the Texas hill country ends. I use the word pond because that's what it is: a manmade reservoir not even seventy feet across at its widest point and never more than fifteen feet deep. Already the shore of the brackish waters, mosquito infested and filmy, is lined with townspeople who are discussing the ship's *strangeness*, wide-eyed gawkers lacking the vocabulary to describe the vessel in better detail. Jeremy Johnson came by just a few minutes ago to ask if I wanted to drive out with him and his father to see it.

"Boys should like boats," my grandad says after I close the front door and come back into the kitchen. He's swishing cold coffee around in his mouth like its water and he's trying to rid himself of a bad taste. "Not cooking. Women cook."

"What about cowboys?" I ask. "They had to cook on the trail."

My grandfather looks up at me, leaning back in his wheelchair. "That ain't trail food." He points to the blue enamel dish with the flour mixture. "That there is beef stroganoff."

I look down at the pieces of beef I'm slicing and see a little blood running off the cutting board onto the counter. When I look up, I see the cracking paint on the cabinet, and I just stare at it. I don't want to go see the boat because I don't really care for boats or for bugs. Mr. Sanders was crazy and everyone knew it and whatever they'd found is, I'm sure, some weirdo project he'd built over the years.

"Those other boys don't call you pussy, do they?" granddad asks, and I know that's a threat.

He's a good ol' boy, from the generation where gender binaries were a way of life so engrained there wasn't even terminology for the way people defined themselves other than male and female. Gender and sex weren't two different things, and he thinks I'm effeminate because I like to cook and would rather read than play football or beat people up. He grew up in a different time, and I try not to fault him. But sometimes it's fucking hard, especially when he's eating the food *I've* cooked.

I inhale deeply through my nose. I count to three and then exhale quietly and slowly. "Do *you* want me to go see the boat?"

"Yes I want you to go see the goddamn boat. Take some goddamn pictures and bring them back." He's picked up his mug and is wheeling, one-handed, towards the coffee maker for a refill.

I know this isn't about me. It's about him. But I don't understand why he just can't be nice. Grandma said you kill more flies with honey than with vinegar. They were married for more than sixty years; I think the phrase should have stuck somewhere in that time.

"Fine I'll go see the boat. If you want me to. Tomorrow."

Granddad nods. "When is dinner gonna be ready?"

*

When I arrive, half the school is out and one-quarter of the town's adults are skipping work, closing shop early, or leaving jobs half done. It's a small town and we can get away with these things when something exciting presents itself.

The mosquitoes are a battalion and I'm fodder. My thumb is already on the shutter button when I step out from between the trees, ready to snap a few photos and head home, and I see the boat.

I figured it would be something other than it is, something akin to a sailboat or speedboat, a recognizable summer vessel. I am not a boat enthusiast and know little about ships, but this is something altogether different, and I can see why the town has turned out to ogle it. It looks like Hollywood dropped a movie prop from the 1940s into the sad excuse for a pond, and then they forgot about it.

The boat is low, and I don't mean just in the water. The deck is low too, but it's three tiers that rise only slightly higher than the last so that the ship looks like it has three long, confused steps. It has three sails too, hanging in tatters from the masts, a plain cream canvas dirtied by years of pond trauma, the wood dark brown and dull.

They mutter, every one of them. *Strange* peppers their sentences. They have no other words and the camera is in my hand, I am looking through the lens, I am snapping picture after picture and wishing I'd brought the camera bag with a lens that could get me closer because I am not going in that water but I want to see the details, the abandonment, the sign that will tell me this is a joke, a crazy man's dream, and not a real ship in a pond in rural Texas.

When there is no more film, I lower the camera and look, like the rest, at the ship that came out of nowhere. When I use the word *displaced*, they quiet and all look at me, and suddenly I am the person to talk to because I've started to describe it, not just comment on it.

"What do you think kid?" Dox shouts from farther down shore, his question like a spear.

I don't answer immediately, and the people are waiting to hear what I'm going to say, like I'm going to give them the answer even though I don't know shit about boats, and suddenly I realize that the mosquitoes aren't even bothering me anymore and I'm the center of attention, some high school nobody whose careless word made it seem like I knew something, *displaced* meaning out of place, in this case, out of place and perhaps the word even implied out of time, which also implied that I knew what time the boat did belong to, and the people are waiting and I am going to lie to them.

"I think it's Spanish." The sentence comes too easily and some people nod like this makes perfect sense. "Or it could be English." History classes have taught me that these countries have traditionally had large navies. "I'll have to think it over."

The explanation is accepted without challenge; someone has at least proposed one small thing to explain an aspect of this *strange* object and even though I didn't bother to say where the ship might have come from, or how old it is, or how it got here, my answer seems like enough and I nod to myself and tap the camera against my thigh. "I'll have to think it over," I say again. "I'll let you know."

I walk back to the road, to my granddad's rusted Cadillac, and leave the town behind me, thinking I know more than they do.

*

At the Market Basket, I wait for the pictures to be developed and eat sunflower seeds and drink cream soda. It's one of the only soft drinks in the place that isn't canned or sold in plastic. I'm picky about what I consume, and I like beverages in glass bottles. They just taste different.

Daniel develops the pictures right away because he hasn't seen the ship yet, and then he asks if he can keep one and I tell him sure, thanks for doing it all so quick. When I get home I slap the packet of pictures down on the table in front of granddad.

"I need to know what kind of ship it is," I tell him.

He looks up at me and I can see how yellow his eyes are; I haven't noticed how cloudy his irises have become until now. He's beginning to look like our old Labrador retriever, Lucy. Her eyes were eventually completely blurred over and she moved around the house slowly, the patterns between furniture memorized but still not trusted.

"Huh," he says.

This is not his normal *huh*, the dismissive *huh*. This is a question *huh* and the word is elongated, curving up at the end.

"I went to see the boat," I tell him. "And it's not a boat. It's a ship. I need to know what kind of ship it is."

"Thought you didn't care about boats," he says, but he's reaching eagerly for the packet anyway, his fingers curling and uncurling as he leans into the table. "What makes you think I'm going to know what this is?" He snorts now, peeling the sticky edge of the envelope back.

Now I *humph*, a sound much like his *huh* only with more skepticism. Grandad used to be navy. Always loved ships. Ever since he was a kid. Has a collection of eleven ships in bottles. Made every one himself from kits he ordered in the mail years back, before grandma died. He turns, dumps the pictures out on the table, and they spread like a fan.

My granddad fumbles for his reading glasses even though the small chain is around his neck; they're where they always are. They still have the +- sticker on them and I don't know why he won't take it off. He picks up one photo. I take a seat in the chair across from him and stare at the back of the paper, the red time and date stamp. He puts down this photo; it is the one I took of the middle mast. He picks up another. He goes through the entire stack very quickly. Then he goes through it again, pausing to study detail, separating the photos into two piles as he critiques them.

I am running out of patience, even though I don't care about ships.

"Well," he finally says, tapping the corner of the photo in his hand on the table. "This sure is...bizarre." I thought he was going to say *strange*, and I feel a small amount of pride that he's managed to avoid the word. "I think..." He stops again, purses his mouth from side to side like he does when he's swishing coffee. He seems to be uncertain of what to say and now he's tapping the photo with his right hand and drumming the fingers of his left on the table. "We need to go to the library."

The closest library is thirty minutes away, but I know my granddad doesn't want to go there. He thinks the librarian (assuming the same one is still there, eating Tums like candy and snorting excessively) is ill-mannered and dumb, and it's a mutual dislike because she doesn't care for my granddad either. Actually, I remember *her* calling *him* ill-mannered the last time we were there, me looking for books on Native Americans for my history class and granddad being "disruptive" and complaining that the newspapers were too wrinkled. We both prefer to go to the larger library, even though it is almost an hour drive.

"Okay," I say, as if this demand is normal and we've been doing errands together for years. And then, more tentatively, I ask, "When do you want to go?"

"Tomorrow," he responds, looking out the kitchen window. He has dropped the picture back onto the table and is rubbing his thighs. I do not know if he is wondering how well his legs will work, or if he's willing them into action. "The sun is going down," he offers as explanation. "Today we'd be too late."

*

The drive is not a pleasant one, but at least granddad isn't complaining. Our shocks are nonexistent as we trampoline through the hills, but we both grin and bear it. He looks out the window and hums to himself songs I don't know. When I turn my head to look at him, he seems smaller than he used to be. Multiple times he begins to say something but no words come out. I become uncomfortable because this is not the granddad I'm used to. The granddad I know is an early 20th-century man: pocket watch, card-playing, cigar-smoking, rough and tumble kind of guy with a sharp tongue and an even sharper wit. This man is quiet and sedate; his face flushes red from time to time.

We park and I get his wheelchair out of the trunk. He folds himself into it and we go up the ramp. I hold the large wooden door open and push him inside. The air is cool and smells musty. A young man in his thirties looks up but I wave him away. My granddad has the pictures in his lap and is rolling the envelope's adhesive off into little brown balls, dropping them onto the carpet as we move along. We locate the card catalog and find a number of books, then take the elevator to the second floor where I try to rationalize the silence between us as therapeutic, not awkward.

When we find the right stacks, the wheelchair won't fit down the thin aisle and so I have to park granddad at an end table. When I return, I divide the books I pulled evenly between us and he splits the photos for us. We begin our comparisons, but not ten minutes in, my granddad is the one who locates the ship after turning pages so furiously I think I've heard him tear a few.

"It's an English Sloop-of-war," he says, pushing the book over to me. I've been reading about a Junk, a Chinese boat with sails that look like wide, deformed fans. I take the book from him and give him mine. One of the ships he has caged in glass is a Junk, I'm sure of it.

I compare the ship in our photos to the illustration in the book. I read that the British Navy used these small, light warships for over two centuries, from the 1500s to the 1700s. My granddad has my book open beside him, but now he is looking at another, flipping through the pages.

"Yeah, this seems right," I say.

My granddad nods at me.

"Aren't you excited?" I ask him. "This thing came out of nowhere and nobody seems to know why or how. It's a total mystery. You just figured it out."

"I didn't figure out shit," he responds. "Got the ship, sure, but we still don't know who put it there or why. Besides, a Sloop-of-war. Not really all that interesting a ship. Psh." When he makes the noise some spittle flies across the table.

"You were interested in this," I say, tapping the photo laid across the page. In all the years since grandma died he's been crotchety and blunt. The library has been the first real request he's made of me in a long time and I don't understand what's happening, first the silence and now the not caring.

"And now I'm interested in *this*," he says, pointing at the book he's been looking at. "A Spanish Galleon. That's a ship."

"And this isn't?"

"I want to make this ship," he responds, changing the conversation. "I want to build this ship in a bottle. It would look good with the others, give me something to do. I wonder if we could get a kit." He's leaning over the page, the dark spots on his scalp exposed from under thin wisps of hair.

"Do you want to see the ship?" I ask, suspecting now the origin of his strange behavior.

He raises his face and looks at me. We both know the path down to the pond isn't something he'll be able to walk. It's a good quarter mile of trail with tree roots and deep ruts. I doubt his wheelchair can make it, but I'm willing to offer.

The swishing again. "Maybe," he says.

"Then we'll figure it out," I tell him.

He rubs his nose and his face is red. "I haven't built a ship in years," he says. "I don't know if I could anymore."

This is the first time in a long time that he has admitted he is unsure of anything, and now, in the span of one minute, he'd muttered two uncertainties.

*

On the way home the car runs out of gas. The floater gauge is broken, and I always have to guess how much is left. I normally don't drive so far but am prepared for this emergency anyway. I always keep a five-gallon jug in the trunk. When I am done emptying the fuel into the tank my hands stink and I'm ready to be home.

"You ever been sailing?" Granddad asks when I get back in the car. The engine chokes once but then the car starts up. He knows I've never been sailing.

"I haven't," I tell him, wondering why he's asking because he knows the answer. The city is falling away and the asphalt curves like a dull snake into the hills.

"No one *sails* anymore," he complains. "All these movie stars and presidents have speed boats. That ain't an art. That's a hobby."

Though my granddad was in the navy, it's a time he doesn't talk about. He shuns the VA hall and calls the men that gather there "sad elephants". Their memories are too long and so are their noses. I know nothing about his life back then.

"You used to sail," I say, half statement, half question.

He harrumphs. "Used to be sailing was an adventure, a way of life. You know they've found Viking settlements in Canada? Came all the way from Scandinavia in their dragon ships. All the way across the Atlantic in those damn small things, four hundred years before Columbus got that cozy job with those carracks and caravels."

I don't think Christopher Columbus and his crew had it easy, but

I'm not going to argue with him. He seems to be getting at something.

"Everything moves too fast," he goes on. "Cars, boats, technology. Wish people would slow down for a damn minute. There," he says, pointing up the road with a shaking hand. Somehow, even with his bad eyes he's spotted the gas station before me. "Filler up."

I gas up the tank, refill the jug. When we get back in the car the fuel gauge reads empty and there is no more conversation.

*

We get back and on the porch is the town *Gazette*, five legal size pieces of paper folded in half and stapled. Our "newspaper" is usually full of other cities' news but today there is a headline that reads "The British are Coming: New England University to Send Researchers to Mystery Ship". The article has been written by John Weathers. Granddad hates John Weathers because John thinks he's a big-time man in a small town. *We're all nobodies*, granddad likes to say, *and we should all know that by now.*

"Bah," he spits as I wheel him into the house. "That place is going to be crawling with people. I don't want to go anymore."

He flicks on the light switch and I mentally note that he never actually said he *did* want to go see the ship. I start getting things out of cabinets, preparing the chicken-fried steak we'll have for dinner. "Yes you do," I say, preheating the oven for the skillet.

"No I don't." He sounds like a child.

"Yes, you do," I say again. "You just don't want people to see you struggle."

I expect him to argue, but he doesn't. "It's embarrassing," he says instead. "I don't want them to see me like this."

It's as if all we needed this whole time was for one of us to say it.

Just one of us to say that four syllable word: embarrassing.

"We could go at night," I suggest. "We could go *to*night."

I turn to look at him. His eyes are wide and shining.

*

We eat dinner in the living room, on old TV tray tables that groan on rusted hinges when I unfold them. When granddad suggested them at first I thought he was joking because he only eats at the table. I had to dig for them in the back of the hall closet, finding them wedged between some of grandma's old coats. So much of her has been put away over the years.

With the TV muted granddad makes me retrieve the ships from his bedroom. I bring them out in four loads, pulled from atop his dresser and nightstands, and set them up in front of us on the coffee table. He tells me the types of ships they are: Junk, Brig, Dromon, Snow, Tern Schooner, Galiote, Fifie, Clipper, Brigantine, Bireme, and my favorite now, a Cutter. I like the Cutter because it has simple, clean lines. It looks like a ship with a purpose, not ostentatious and overbearing. Granddad tells me about the process of assembling a ship in a bottle and does not complain one time about my cooking, a usual evening routine.

"Long tweezers," he says. He is mashing up peas into a paste with his fork. "A steady hand. Assemble the pieces inside with little dots of superglue. Sometimes people put them together outside so it's collapsible-like. Then they use a string to pull the masts up once it's inside. That's cheating though."

"How long does it take?" I hold the Cutter up to the light.

"Don't get gravy on that!" he warns. "It depends…I was never in any hurry."

"We could make one," I suggest. "You could start it."

"Maybe. Maybe," he contemplates, but he is shaking his head yes.

"Is there a way to make fake water or something?" I ask him.

"I'm sure there is."

"Could we make a Sloop-of-war?"

"If there's a kit for it."

"I'll find one."

After dinner we leave the dishes in the sink and I phone Mr. Weathers on speakerphone and tell him my granddad and I know what type of ship it is. Mr. Weathers says, "What in the world is a schloomp?" and I tell him he can do his own research if he doesn't believe me and hang up on him. Granddad laughs and slaps his knees as if I've just told some grand joke.

We watch the evening news and then a sitcom that neither of us knows. When the town is silent and sleeping, we leave the house and start the car. Granddad lights a cigar with his navy lighter and smokes out the window; it's a cigar he's been saving for the day he dies, he claims. And though this makes no sense, I don't tell him to stub it out. It's been three years since he smoked. The doctors told him he had to quit, and he did. He had.

We park and turn the headlights off. There is a full moon and his wheelchair is rickety on the path. "Good, good," he says when I make it over a large root with a grunt. It takes much longer than I thought it would, and granddad is not pushing me to go any faster. I think he's enjoying this adventure more than me, even with all the teeth-shattering bumps and near tip-overs.

When we reach the tree line, he lets the dangling branches drag across his face and closes his eyes.

"Okay," I tell him. "Open them."

He does and inhales sharply. He says, "Radiant." Not *strange*, or even *beautiful*, or *extraordinary*. Radiant. Shining. Overwhelming. It is the perfect word. "But a tad dilapidated," he adds.

I laugh. That is an understatement.

The ship is crammed in this pond, like a ship in a bottle. It does not belong here and never has. This water is not ocean water, and there is no crew to take care of her.

"Must weigh fifty tons." My grandfather whispers. "But it's got no sea room. Couldn't maneuver it even if we wanted to. I wish I could swim out to it."

This ship has us both. This crumbling monstrosity, this massive fractured shell is what we've been waiting for our whole lives. I crouch on my heels next to the wheelchair and take my granddad's hand. "It's ours," I tell him. "It's ours."

"And we should burn it."

We don't have to talk about it. I understand what he's saying: that no one should know why this boat is here, no one but us. To everyone else it's only a *thing*, strange and unsettling.

I walk back to the car alone and get the gas can and then my granddad's lighter, still sitting on the dashboard. When I come back, I strip off my shirt and pants and shoes. My granddad folds my clothes and holds them in his lap while I swim out to the boat through swarms of mosquitoes and gnats, holding the lighter in my mouth and floating the gas can in my right hand beside me. I am kicking to stay afloat and know now what's like to have failing legs.

I surprise myself when I climb up the side of the ship so easily. I might be a born sailor and not even know it. I maneuver around like it's my own home. I cover the dry wood with gas but have to try a dozen times before it will light. When it does, it is slow to spread, not like in movies where flames race towards destruction. I scamper down the side, fall into the water, swim back to shore smiling and out of breath. In my damp clothes I stand beside my granddad and we watch the Sloop-of-war burn. Burn like it should have centuries ago on the ocean when at war. We can just barely smell the smoke, even though the wide, dark plumes completely obscure the sky.

THE WORM GIRL

I am wiping fog from the mirror and the blurred image of another girl is looking back, her blonde hair piled loose atop her head. This is why I hate mirrors. Like it's not bad enough staring at your own ugly reflection. It's my luck that someone pretty always comes in before me, leaving her reflection in the glass for me to find—an uninvited competition. I wonder if pretty girls come in *after* me. If *my* reflection makes them feel better about themselves, as I fade, replaced with their own face.

I'm counting down as I wipe the mirror with my towel—four, three, two—and see the girl has red-rimmed eyes. And then she is me: swollen nose, bruise forming on one side. That's what I get for taking advice about how to shoot a bow.

Colleen appears beside me. She smells like antiseptic and cherries and her shower caddy is crammed full of matching products: shampoo, conditioner, bath gel, lotion. She got it in a box our first day at camp. As if anyone needs a care package the first day. Show off.

"Looks bad," she says, her eyes in the mirror angled at me.

Colleen was the one who told me "how" to use the bow. She and I first met a few years ago at camp, but last summer we parted on bad terms when I kissed her summer boyfriend at the dance the final night. I'd forgotten all about Derek's chapped lips, but Colleen hadn't.

"Did you see her?" I ask, nodding to the mirror.

"No."

The reflections only last about ten seconds. Just enough time to get a look, to start scrutinizing the face, before *poof*. Just enough time for me to have seen beyond the delicate nose to the girl's scalp, the gash on her forehead near her hairline.

"You hear about anyone *else* getting injured?" I ask.

"Nope." Colleen pops open her facial moisturizer and leans in.

"Well, we're the first cabin in here today. Maybe it happened last night."

Colleen is looking at her own nose. It seems thinner this year. I wonder if she had a nose job or if she just grew into it. Then she runs a comb through her hair. Cherry scented detangler too. When she walks away, she leaves her reflection. It is smiling at me.

*

In the bathroom, after breakfast, the girl is in the mirror again.

My eyes go first to that cut on her scalp. Was it bruised before too? I don't know.

This girl doesn't pluck her eyebrows. The right one is all fucked up, hairs too long like she slept on them and didn't fix the strays before she went out for the day.

When *I* lean in, *she* leans in. There's something in her eye. A red mote, like a heart turned to five o'clock, floating next to her iris.

Worm Girl comes in, toothbrush in hand. She brushes her teeth after every meal, not just morning and night.

"Hey," I say, and she nods back at me.

Worm Girl's been coming to Lake Ranch since she was in grade school, the only other person cast into this hell hole every single year of her youth besides me, both our parents eager for some time alone. Every summer, without fail, Worm Girl shows up with a trunk of khaki clothes and a fly-fishing vest. We don't go fly fishing at Lake Ranch. We don't do any fishing; the lake we swim in is man-made and dyed an awful green.

Worm Girl doesn't make friends. I saw her try that first summer here, but this is camp for girls who like ribbons and dresses and stickers, not a camp for girls who like jungles and dirt. It's not for girls who brush their teeth *after* breakfast; it's for girls who get bronze in tanning beds, their teeth glowing with UV bleaching products.

The reflection she leaves after meals always has a bit of toothpaste on her lip. Sometimes, after she's gone, I try to wipe it away.

*

The third day of camp is the all-camp campout. Real wilderness shit. Roasting marshmallows and making s'mores. Burning marshmallows and catching twigs attached to marshmallows on fire. Ghost stories.

Sam isn't roasting marshmallows. She's eating just the chocolate bar instead.

"You're not doing it right," Colleen says.

"Fuck off," Sam says, grabbing the marshmallow Colleen's just put on her stick and throwing it into the fire. "Fetch."

Cara laughs.

There's whiskey in their apple cider. Cara has the flask shoved in her underwear and she has to lean back against the log Sam's sitting on in order to smooth the line of her figure, or else the flask's metal top digs into her ribs.

"God you are *such* a *bitch*." Colleen walks off, tossing her empty stick into the bonfire.

"She doesn't need any more sugar anyway," Cara says. "Sugar will make her fat."

I doubt anything will make Colleen fat, but I keep my mouth shut. I like Cara and Sam because they've got no filters. I wish I could be like that, suck it up, never worry about what people think of me—

free to say whatever I want. It would be easier than trying to master teenage politics.

The Worm Girl is a few logs away from us. By herself. Her marshmallow is on fire and she's just watching it char.

"What's her deal?" Cara asks.

"Maybe she likes carcinogens," Sam suggests. "Pyromania can be a sign of sexual frustration. Maybe she can't stand being away at camp for a week. Maybe back home she's got a boyfriend and they fuck like rabbits."

"Ooh, ooh!" Cara tries to sit up. Leans back again. "Maybe she's got a whole secret life at home. She's like, steampunk or goth, or like, a dungeons and dragons nerd. The *only* girl nerd…"

I like the idea that the Worm Girl is only Worm Girl here at Lake Ranch. I hope her nickname hasn't followed her home.

"And she's got a *huge* vagina," Sam offers. "That's why she has to wear those baggy safari shorts."

"You guys. Cut it out," I say.

"Or she's a lesbian," Cara says.

The two burst into fits of laughter. I know the Worm Girl can hear us.

I get up and go to sit by her. "They're just being stupid."

"I know." She blows out her marshmallow. "Besides, these shorts are Steve Irwin limited edition. Hard to get. High fashion for certain crowds."

"Really?"

"No. But it sounds good."

I've never heard the Worm Girl make a joke and it passes so suddenly I don't even laugh.

Denise, our counselor, arrives with the speaking stick. It's really just a dowel rod with yarn and feathers attached to it. She raps it on the ground. "It's time. Time," she proclaims, "for planning the Telling of Tales."

She might be a bit drunk too for all I know. Most of the counselors are college students and at night they sneak out and drink, make out, have sex. I've always wondered why there's no security guard, how the admin hasn't figured out what's going on. Or maybe the admin does know and doesn't care.

"You coming?" I ask the Worm Girl.

"Have you read *The Portrait of Dorian Grey*?"

"Uh…I don't think so."

She nods her head as if she expected that answer. "No, I'm not going. Ghost stories are for children."

She's right, but it's a camp tradition. Once you're old enough to be in a senior cabin you spend the first few days with the other cabin-mates making up a ghost story for the Telling of Tales competition. The past three years Colleen and her groupies have finagled it so that they're always in charge of our cabin's narrative.

"Okie dokie, then."

I help Cara get up, and Sam trails behind us, grabbing a bag of abandoned marshmallows at the s'mores station and shoving three in her mouth all at once.

The big bonfire is on the lake's narrow beach, and we sit on the far side. Colleen tosses her hair and pushes us to use her story about a crazy man whose ghost murders campers. Sam still argues for her tale about a camp full of ghosts—children left to starve and cannibalize each other when their parents decide they'd rather not have their kids back.

Sam's story does not win the vote for the ghost story we'll use at the Telling of Tales, but this doesn't stop her from yelling *all* her ideas at the other girls in our cabin as they begin working out the details of Colleen's narrative.

"Morons!" Sam says, kicking dirt in their direction. "You don't know anything about what's scary!"

*

The girl is in the mirror again. The bruise on her head has spread a purple blotch along her hairline. Her reflection leans towards me and her mouth is open, inspecting the socket where a tooth should be.

"Do you guys fucking see this?" I ask.

Sam is peeing with the stall door open, but she can't see the mirror. Cara leans over and catches just a glimpse before the girl's reflection disappears. "Whoa. What happened to *her*?"

"Do you recognize her?"

Cara shakes her head. "Never seen her."

"What's going on?" Sam steps out of the stall and pulls toilet paper from the bottom of her shoe while I give her the rundown about the mysterious mirror girl.

"It's like, we should *know* who she is," I say. "There aren't *that* many campers."

"Maybe she's a counselor," Cara suggests.

I shake my head.

"Maybe she's not a part of the camp." Sam gets a blackhead strip from her bag.

"So what would she be doing out here in the middle of BFE if she's not part of the camp?"

"Running. Maybe it's like that horror movie where people are hunting the tourists and she's trying to get away."

"Gross," Cara says. "That's not funny."

"Do you think we should tell someone?" I ask. "I've seen her like, three times now. Whoever she is, she's *here*, camper or not."

"Actually," Cara says, "maybe you *should* say something."

"Y'all worry too much." Sam says and turns to leave.

We both look at Sam as she walks out, then her reflection in the mirror, head cocked to the side, smiling to show wide, white teeth.

*

My discussion with the admin does not go well. Moira is too old to be here, and I think it colors her interaction with me. While most of the counselors are college kids, Moira is like, thirty-five. Her clothes are a cross between matron and tween: high-waisted pants and neon accessories. I think she gets off on being in charge because camp is the only place where she means anything.

"Everyone's accounted for," she tells me from across her desk. The AC blows hard, rattling in the wooden window frame.

"Maybe she's not a camper," I suggest. "People live around here, right? She might need help."

For a second Moira seems to consider this, but then she says, "What do you want me to do, call the cops? Crimes don't happen at Lake Ranch. We run a safe show."

On the way back to my cabin I see the Worm Girl by the side of the road, frog-squatting with a stick in the mud.

"What are you doing?" I ask.

"Taking care of things."

I see that she's helping an earthworm find its way off the cement.

"They'll die in the sun," she explains. "They breathe through the mucus on their skin and when they dry up they suffocate."

"That's kind of weird."

"No, they're really cool actually. A lot of archaeological finds are preserved by them. Really powerful little guys. And *this* one," she says, "has a long way to go…" She uses the stick to cover him with wet dirt once he's found his way to safety.

"So…it's not the destination, it's the journey? Is that how it goes?"

"Don't cheapen it like that," she says, but Worm Girl doesn't sound angry. If anything, what she's said sounds commonplace, like she's said it over and over again and now it's just slightly chiding, mostly annoyance.

"Sorry. Just trying to get it."

"Have you ever seen what a geode looks like before it's cracked open?"

"No."

"For going to one of the best schools, I'd think you'd know something like that."

"How do you know where I go to school?"

"Facebook."

I'm not sure if I should be flattered or creeped out by what she's said. I've never once thought to search Facebook for Worm Girl. Not that I'd be able to anyway with a name like Worm Girl. What is her real name? Jenny? Emily?

"Where do you go?" I ask. "Local?"

"Regular school. Public. You know I took the test to get into your school. Passed it. They offered me a scholarship and everything."

"Really? You turned it down?"

"I went for my visit. You know Wendy Watts? She was my student guide. I saw you that day. Playing soccer. I would have played too but no one told me to bring gym clothes, so I just sat in the stands and watched the whole time."

Too late and the question is out of my mouth. "Why didn't you say hi?"

We both know why.

"You know you can find parts of meteors around here," she goes on. "Most people don't even know what to look for, but they're everywhere."

I pride myself on trying to be nice. I'm no Wendy Watts, head of the school's leadership committee, but I do charity work. The thing about being nice though, is that it's easy to be nice *if* the reason is right. It's easy to pass out sandwiches on cheap white bread with Miracle Whip when you get to go home to something better. It's easy to be nice when you're tutoring another student in biology because it's really just studying to you, the girl who's going to make an A anyway. It's easy to be nice when there's nothing at stake.

"Why didn't you say hi?" I ask again because I need her to say it.

"Really?" She looks at me, standing up, stick still in her hand.

"Yeah, really." I wouldn't have ignored her.

"We're not friends."

"But I would have said hi back." And I would have, the polite thing to do. We may not be friends but we're not enemies. She's not Colleen.

"You know this year is the first year you've actually talked to me more than two times?"

I would have talked to you, I want to say. *I would have said hi.* I'm not a bad person. "Did you decide not to come to my school because of me?"

She shakes her head. "It would have been too inconvenient for my parents. The school is, like, 30 minutes from my house and they both work."

"There's a ride share."

"Wendy told me. But no one was close to me. Wouldn't work out." She turns the stick over in her hands. "You know I met this guy once, in Santa Fe, and he was a meteor hunter. Had a back room in his store full of fossils and stuff that weren't for sale. He showed them to me and while we were in there some tourists came down the stairs and he was clearly mad they they'd caught us. I mean, we weren't doing anything. I just think he was mad that some people saw that stuff when he hadn't invited them to. Like his privacy had been invaded."

"They could have worked it out," I say. "They don't just give scholarships to anyone."

"You know what he told me later? He told me some people just don't get it. They walk around so oblivious and think things are interesting for half a second until something else comes along. He said they had no clue what he had to go through to have what he had. I think about that sometimes when I find something worth keeping. All the things I had to get through or do to find it. People don't think about history. They only think about now."

*

Sam screams on her way down towards the blob—the giant inflatable cushion floating in the lake. When she hits, it's a wet smacking noise.

"Ouch," Cara winces. "I don't think she meant to do a belly flop."

We're sitting on the island—a barge with lawn chairs and a railing with squirt guns attached. The boys have been out already, and they've left the place a mess of coke cans and candy bar wrappers. The Worm Girl is picking it all up, shoving it all inside a t-shirt she's fashioned like a trash bag, tying the holes at the head and arms into small, tight knots.

She wears a black two-piece with gold trim. She looks like she's beginning to burn, her shoulders red. When she looks at me, I hold up the bottle of sunscreen and she comes to take it from me without a word, rubbing the thick paste into her pale skin.

Colleen and her friends are swinging out across the monkey bars, trying and failing to reach the golden ticket, a laminated piece of yellow paper that hangs from a bar just past the last rung. Whoever gets the golden ticket wins a special dessert for his or her cabin the last night of camp. Every year, a guy snags it.

Colleen has a swimmer's body, long and lean. Her shoulders strain as she swings—reaches—misses—and tries again. What I wouldn't give for arms like those.

Sam hoists herself up onto the barge, rocking it so that the rest of the girls shoot her dirty looks. The Worm Girl hands the lotion back to me and returns to collecting trash.

"I am so done with this place," Sam says, taking an empty chair. Her midsection is red from where she hit the blob. "Wish we had a TV."

Colleen slips from the bars and splashes into the lake. Her friends moan.

"Hey Worm Girl," Sam says, "Think you can get it?" She nods towards the golden ticket.

"Sam," I say. "Stop it."

"What?" Sam feigns innocence.

"Maybe," the Worm Girl says, eying the bars. I think it's the first time she's ever spoken to Sam. "Think *you* can?"

"Is that a challenge?" Sam asks.

The Worm Girl nods.

Our stupid non-counselor Denise isn't paying us any attention. I think she's asleep on her towel with her sunglasses on.

Sam gets up and heads to the edge of the barge, Colleen's cronies parting for her. When she reaches out for the first rung the barge begins to rock—Colleen climbing up the ladder with more force than necessary.

"Oops," she says.

"Dumb bitch," Sam mutters, getting her balance. She reaches again and catches the bar with her right hand, then throws her other arm out, catching the next, and trekking across them like a ninja until she gets to the end where she hangs, swinging slightly. When she reaches, she slips almost immediately and goes down into the water.

"Well there goes that," Cara says.

The Worm Girl walks to the bars.

"C'mon," Sam calls from the water. "Do it."

From behind, the Worm Girl's back looks splotchy. I can see where she hasn't been able to reach, the sunscreen shining but the middle of her back matte. Her hands are shaking at her sides.

She steps to the edge and reaches out. She kind of falls forward, but pulls one arm up in time to grab the first bar. There she hangs, limp. She tries to swing, to get some momentum to reach the next rung.

I can't help but think she *looks* like a worm hanging from a fishhook, the way her body seems to twist up on itself, flailing. A pale little flesh-colored worm squirming in the sun.

She doesn't make it to the next bar. She can't hold her own weight, and on the backswing, she slips, letting go, her head smacking the fake grass edge of the barge on the way down.

Colleen screams.

Denise says, "What's going on?"

*

"I fucking thought she was dead," Cara says.

Sam hasn't said a word. She knows I'm angry, I think. That, or she's embarrassed and doesn't want to admit she was a bitch.

I guess Denise isn't as worthless as I thought because she jumped right in, turned the Worm Girl over so she wouldn't drown, and flagged the lifeguard.

"You shouldn't have pushed her to do that," I say to Sam. "That was really fucking mean."

"I know," Sam finally says.

We're in line for the shower, and when it's my turn I scrub off the sunscreen until my arms are pink and raw. And then I keep scrubbing, long after the sunscreen is gone. Then I crouch at the bottom of the shower and let the water pelt my head.

"Are you coming?" Cara calls.

"In a minute."

When the bathroom is quiet, I finally come out. Cara's reflection is in the mirror. She isn't smiling or brushing her hair or anything. It's just Cara, her eyes looking to the stall I'd just occupied.

The bruise on the side of my nose is starting to spread to my cheek, and it's turning green. Green is good. It means it's healing. I wonder if the mysterious mirror girl's face is healing too, and I wonder what happened to her tooth. I haven't seen her since my meeting with Moira. No one has.

The Worm Girl comes in and sees me standing at the mirror.

"You okay?" I ask.

"Yeah."

"Concussion?"

"No. I didn't pass out. Was just sort of stunned and couldn't swim. I panicked."

She's still in her bikini. I wonder what happened to her trash bag shirt.

"You know," she says. "Sometimes I come in here and it's your reflection in the mirror. You're never smiling."

I haven't thought about that, but I don't doubt her. I don't ever walk away happy with the way I look. Why would I smile?

"I always make sure to come in when someone else is here," she says, turning on the water. "That way, another person always uses the mirror after me—my reflection doesn't get stuck in there for hours waiting for someone to replace it."

"They're just reflections. They don't have feelings."

"I know. That's not what bothers me."

*

In the night I wake when I hear scuffling. Denise, I assume, coming back from a rendezvous.

But the door is on the far end of the room and what I'm hearing echoes along the wall beside my bunk. The plywood reverberates with it.

When I sit up, I see Sam beside the Worm Girl's bed.

"What's going on?" another girl asks.

The Worm Girl is quivering under her sheets. "She's having a seizure," Sam says, bending down. "She's having a seizure! Someone call 911!"

"Shit." I get out of bed and rush to them.

Colleen's face is ghostly in her cell phone's light.

"She's not here!" the girl yells. "Where the fuck is Denise?"

"Try to turn her on her side," I say.

I'm out the door, my feet on the path, rocks digging into my soles. I keep saying *Oh God, Oh God*, until the words become my breathing. In, *Oh*. Out, *God*.

There is no sound—no crickets, no bugs, no bats. Fucking Denise and these goddamn kids in charge of this place.

The lights in Moira's cabin are on. There are shadows on the porch. I try to yell but I can't catch my breath.

Then I see her. The girl.

She is standing between me and the cabin, just off the path, between two trees. She looks like a wild woman, her hair tangled, her legs bare and scraped. She isn't wearing any pants, just a white t-shirt, underwear, and tennis shoes.

She puts her finger to her lips. *Shhh.*

"Worm Girl!" I yell, and the shadows around Moira's cabin swivel towards me. "She's having a seizure."

Moira is one of the shadows. She unpeels herself from the darkness and yells, "Who is that?"

"Seizure," I yell again. "Cabin 12!"

A string of curses comes from the porch and then I'm running again, back to the Worm Girl, Moira and some man I don't know at my side.

When I turn to look back the girl from the mirror is gone.

*

The ambulance takes the Worm Girl away. Afterwards, none of us can sleep so we huddle on our bunks, looking out the windows where police lights turn the bark of trees blue and red. The cops are talking to Denise and Moira outside. We can't hear what they're saying.

Even after Denise comes back in, her face wet with tears, we cannot sleep. She will not talk to us, *can't*, she says.

Colleen glares at her. "I'm calling my parents."

"Go ahead," Denise says, hand on the doorknob to her mini-room. "Cops were going to do it anyway." With that, she closes her door behind her.

"At least she's not dead," Sam says to me.

The three of us are on my bed.

"Fuck," Cara says. "I gotta dump out that whiskey."

I know I should be thinking about the Worm Girl, but I can only think about the other girl, wild in the woods.

We sit until the sun comes up, none of us really talking, and by the time breakfast is served parents are already showing up—cars jamming the parking lot of the main office.

While I eat cereal my mom calls and says she talked to the Sheriff last night. *Is everyone okay?* she wants to know. *We're coming to get you. That place isn't safe.*

By the time the meal is done, Sam has gone. No goodbye. Nothing.

Cara says her mom is coming. A few hours.

The cabins are emptying out. The cops are still here, overseeing the shutdown. We hear words like *MIP, marijuana, cocaine.*

Cara and I walk to the lake. The blob is forgotten; the barge floats on still waters. On it I can see the Worm Girl's shirt, still bloated with garbage. I wonder who will come to pick up her things.

"This is just…so weird."

"I know," I say. "You think I should go get it?"

"What?"

"Her shirt."

Cara's cheeks flush red. "I mean the camp shutting down. Now that I think about it, I wonder how it's been running at all."

"Moira?" I say.

"Yeah. But she can't own it, right? She's too young. You've been here every year, right? Haven't you ever seen a bigwig?"

"Not that I know of. But you know, the camp has been on the decline since…" I try to think, try to remember the year when things changed. "Well, when Moira came in, I guess. About four years ago."

"What do you think will happen to people in the kitchen and stuff?"

"Probably nothing. This is like, what, one week out of the summer? I'm sure they have other jobs."

"Yeah."

We stare out at the lake, at the shirt on the barge. Only now do I see the distinctive camp logo on the fabric, the outline of a cabin and three lazy blue lines below it. That shirt was from three years ago. The Worm Girl had won it when there used to be raffles.

"Cara? Cara Garboza?"

A cop is walking towards us.

"One of your last names is Garboza?" he calls.

"Did you ever dump that whiskey?" I whisper, afraid that the cop is coming because of that, relieved that he stops to listen to something on his radio.

"Yeah. This morning. You know, I saw that girl in the mirror. The one you've been seeing. Did you ever find out what happened with that?"

"No. Moira said it was nothing."

"Garboza?" he calls again, and Cara raises her hand.

"Can you imagine what it would be like to be her? Moira, I mean. Seeing your own reflection just waiting for you all the time? Like in that shitty little cabin and it's the first thing you see in the morning and the last thing at night? Ugh. At least we have each other."

The cop says Cara's parents are here. When she leaves she promises to friend me on Facebook.

"Why didn't you find me last summer?" I ask.

"Camp friends," she says, as if it explains everything.

My parents are some of the last to arrive. When they find me, I'm sitting in the cabin. I've packed the Worm Girl's things, but no one's shown up for them.

They look disheveled. My mother's hair isn't styled, and my father's shirt is wrinkled.

"We can't just leave it here," I say, pointing at Worm Girl's trunk.

"They'll come for it," my mother tells me, but even she looks unsure.

The cop looks done with the whole camp fiasco, his shoulders slumped. "Is someone coming for this?" I ask.

"I can't say."

The trunk is open. I've gotten her toiletries from the bathroom.

There was no wild girl in the mirror—no Worm Girl either. It was Colleen I saw last, her hand pressing against her headband, frowning.

"They'll call, right?" I ask. "They'll call her parents?"

The cop nods.

I don't know why I'm so reluctant to leave. Lake Ranch is a broken piece of shit and nothing good happens here.

My father gets my bag and my mother puts her arm around my shoulders. "Are *you* okay?" she asks.

"Yeah. I just gotta use the bathroom."

My mother waits for me outside.

There's no toilet paper, so I use paper towel. I look at myself in the mirror and realize what my mother must have thought: that something terrible happened to me here. I'd forgotten about the bruise. When I touch my face, it doesn't even hurt.

With Lake Ranch closing shop I wonder how long it will be before someone else comes in here. Days. Weeks. Months. Years. I don't want to leave my reflection here that long. I don't want to leave it frozen in the glass, staring at toilets and empty shower stalls. I try different expressions—smiling for one—but they all look manufactured and fake. Finally I give up, close my eyes, and turn away.

AFTER THE STORM

The newspaper article said two people died, not three. And that's because three people did *not* die, at least not in that car at that time, but the article didn't even mention the boy. The article should have said that Alice and Charles were survived by their pre-teen son, and that the boy now lived up a ladder in the cramped space inside the oversized stingray looming above the gift shop across from the ocean. But of course, it didn't say this because almost no one knew the boy existed. There was no record of him in hospital documents, no social security card or birth certificate. His mother urged him out of her womb in an Arkansas Hot Spring and his father cut the umbilical cord with a butterfly knife sterilized by a zippo's blue flame, and they called the boy Elias, and took him all over the country until their van slipped into the ocean.

*

Elias wondered how hot it would get inside the stingray once Florida was in full summer. He already sweat during the day, felt like he was slowly being cooked inside an easy bake oven he'd once seen advertised on a motel television. But he'd stolen enough beach blankets to line the metal-bellied floor, and because the stingray hung over the edge of the gift shop's roof, it was too high for anyone to see its hatch propped open with a disembodied cooler lid. From inside he looked out the stingray's window eyes and saw the store owner's daughter kissing the blonde surfer boy in the dawn light. The two had spent the night together under lifeguard tower 17 and she'd silenced her phone every time it quacked like a duck.

Her hands were pulling at the surfer boy's hair and he had her pinned against the stucco wall.

Elias thought it must be nice to be needed, instead of needing.

When Amanda pushed her boyfriend away, the two teenagers stood like gasping fools and then she took keys from her pocket to unlock the back door of the souvenir shop. Elias watched the boy walk down the street and kick a stray can before getting into his van.

He crawled out of the hatch and then down the rickety ladder. He knocked on the door five times and wrapped his arms around himself to wait. Eventually, Amanda opened it.

"Hey, Elias." She leaned against the frame and he could see oblong darknesses under her eyes. They looked like mussel shells.

"Hey." He stood for a moment, then said, "Do you have any water?"

He entered the store behind her. The morning was filtering in through the tinted windows and he followed her to the drink cooler where she pulled a bottle out and tossed it to him. His hands slipped on the condensation and it fell, rolling under a rack of badly manufactured t-shirts with too-wide shoulders, finally coming to a stop below a display of stuffed sea creatures. They were piled atop each other near the front door, and Elias could see that they were sun-bleached. Killer whales, dolphins, sea turtles, sharks. All faded and dusty.

"You been doing okay?" Amanda looked him over and then went to flick on the overhead lights.

Elias squinted against the brightness. "Yeah, sure." While her back was turned, he shoved a caramel candy bar into his pocket.

"God, sometimes I just *wish*," she said. "You got it so good. No one telling you what to do, or how to act. No stupid school. Who needs school, you know?"

It was Amanda's dream to leave Florida for LA. She was destined not to be an actress, but a celebrity psychic, and she knew she didn't need high school or college or her father in order to be that.

"I'm so tired of this place," she continued. "Look at this stupid junk."

Elias did look, but he didn't see junk. The souvenir store, though much larger, reminded him of home. The back of the VW van was also crammed with things, tchotchkes his mother called them: something from every place where they spent any significant amount of time. A laminated paper coaster from a diner where his father was a short order cook, a souvenir pen in the shape of the Washington Monument, a needlework pillowcase of the Liberty Bell.

He fingered a whole opened clam shell and tipped it so the googly eyes rolled to the side. His thumbnail caught on a lump of dried glue. "It could be worse."

"Yeah? How?" She opened the register to fiddle with the receipt tape.

"You could be in a van at the bottom of the ocean."

"Whoa, Elias." Amanda lapsed into a fit of laughter. When she looked at him again her cheeks were red splotches. "What a thing to say! Yeah, okay, I guess it could be worse."

Outside a few people were beginning to appear on the street.

"What are you going to do today?" she asked. "Be a king of a sand-castle? Train seals to pull your chariot across the ocean?"

This was Elias' favorite part of the day. Monday through Saturday the two would each proclaim what grand action was going to be performed.

"The seagulls are naming a new emperor," he told her. "I bet it's going to be me, and I've got great ideas about how to fix the litter on the beach and ways to make French fries less salty. I'll live in a mansion overlooking the sea and every day they'll bring me ice cream and magazines. You?"

Amanda's eyes got dull the way they did when she imagined her life outside of the small town. "Have you ever heard of selkies?" she asked, and Elias shook his head no. "They're seals that are really people. The seal skin is just like a second skin, but they can take it off and step out of it and look like, normal."

"That's pretty cool."

"Today I'm going to be a selkie." She fingered her hair and narrowed her eyes. "Today I'm going to take off my skin."

The statement made Elias shiver. "So you're going to be a seal?" he asked.

"Not a seal, just, something else."

Elias thought she either didn't want to complete the thought or couldn't.

"Hey, if you clean the windows, I'll give you three dollars," she said, shifting the conversation.

"Okay." Elias thought of the ice cream store and its forty-two flavors. He wondered how much ice cream cost.

She told him he had twenty minutes and gave him a spray bottle and a dirty rag, stiff in the middle with long-dried cleaning solution. He only got half the windows done; he was too short to clear the tops, and because he'd never cleaned a window before in his life, he left broad streaks of Windex arcing across the glass. Amanda gave him five dollars from the drawer and let him pick a knickknack from the store. He picked a red baseball hat from the discount bin. It was only a little bit too big.

*

A waffle cone with one scoop cost $2.13. Elias sat under a canopied picnic bench near the beach and the funky monkey banana, pecan, and caramel ice cream dripped out the bottom of the cone and ants collected at his feet. He had $2.87 left and he knew later he'd buy a hot dog from the guy who pushed a cart down the sidewalk near the temporary carnival. It was only two dollars. He felt good for the first time in days.

He heard a couple talking about the hurricane. The sea didn't look any different to Elias though. Somewhere out there his parents had drowned, and he licked his fingers while he thought about it. He told himself they must have been sleeping, and then he invented a story about mermaids who tried to rescue them, diving down with conch shells full of air and pulling open the van's doors. If the last thing they saw were mermaids, it probably didn't hurt when they died.

From where he sat, he could see the protected section of the beach. Part of the sands were roped off and signs hung that read *DO NOT ENTER* and *Caution: Protected Sand Crabs*. Someone came by and dumped what was left of their cooler into the trash and Elias pretended to pull something out of his pocket as if to throw that away too. Then he pretended to change his mind, shaking his head as he reached into the trash, his fingers quickly finding half a turkey and cheddar sandwich which he ate as he climbed down the dunes to the beach to watch as the crabs worked tiny wonders with their claws. Amanda told him that once a year the crabs migrated here; they threw themselves into currents and pinched dark waters all the way along the coast until they came to Florida where they fought their way onto the beach and began the process of building elaborate sand castles in which to birth their young.

He knew a little about crabs. The town library was small but with years of traveling and limited space in the van his mother had taught him how to navigate a card catalogue and he could find, with no help, almost anything he wanted. The crabs on the beach were technically called Plotter Crabs. They were a protected species and dwindling fast; the town didn't advertise their presence much because of this. Elias had read that in 1993 some college kids on spring break got drunk and stomped down the half-built crab castles and almost wiped them out.

He knew the baby crabs attached to the underside of the mother crab and that they looked like eggs but weren't. While most crabs release their little ones into the ocean, these crabs raised them in their sand-castles for a few weeks until the babies could fend for themselves. Each female had her own castle, built for her in a collaborative effort of the male crabs vying for her post-mating affections.

The male crabs combined architectural styles with reckless aban-don and an observer might witness what looked to be a basic English medieval castle, square with full crenelated walls, combined with spi-raled towers and bay windows. Or Japanese Shiro with sweeping roofs and a French portcullis. Some castles had no recognizable attributes governed by any period or place, castles made of half-formed fairy tales with rectangular windows at odd intervals and flat roofs with geometric designs.

The female crabs mainly came out at night, and in the moonlight when he wandered the beach, Elias had been able to see them appraising their homes, giving indistinct orders with waving claws and sending their wishful husbands to work. But he'd stopped coming down to see them since he saw one pair of crabs mating, stuck together, and when he returned the next day, found them both dead in the sand, their castle collapsed into two halves.

A few cars pulled up and men began unloading equipment Elias didn't recognize. He grew bored when the male crabs scuttled away into the shelter of their castles, so he wandered the beach looking for sea glass. One thing he used to have, that was his and his alone, was a mayonnaise jar with the label washed off full of rounded and dull glass of all colors. His mother wrote their locations with a thin point permanent marker on the bits and pieces and he'd made a game with them: somewhat like solitaire but instead of suits he judged the pairings with colors and shapes.

He'd been looking for sea glass when his parents sent him away—they did this often—with the important mission of finding the answer to a riddle. What kind of tree fits in your hand? Elias didn't know much about trees. Cactus yes, and flowers, but he figured he didn't have to *know* about trees to see what was small enough to be carried back to the van.

The night his parents disappeared was also the first night he saw Amanda. She was with the tall boy lounging near the entrance to a traveling carnival. She was unwinding purple cotton candy with her mouth and her eyeliner was so thick she looked like a raccoon. Elias liked the look of her; she seemed undone somehow, or unconcerned. Her bones didn't fight her posture and her eyes moved slowly. He wondered what it would be like to become a wave. He walked behind her and her boyfriend on his way back to the van. He saw them stop in front of the souvenir store and looked past them to the families doing their last shopping. A giant inflatable palm tree was being batted by a child who looked to be having a fit, and Amanda made a comment about how she was never going to have kids because they couldn't behave, not even in her store.

Right after she went inside Elias figured out the answer to the riddle. A palm tree. That's the kind of tree that fits in your hand. He laughed when it struck him, and he skipped down the streets all the way to the beach where the van was parked on the sand. Only there was no van. He knew where it had been left, there was an indentation in the dune behind it that looked like a giant footprint, but the sand that had been dry and loose hours before was now compact and wet with the outgoing tide.

That night the windows of the souvenir shop glowed with blue and white lava lamps and nightlights decorated with sea shells. He didn't know who he might ask for help and was scared of what might happen to him without his parents. The stingray awning above the front door had eyes that glowed too, and he could see the small space inside: metal beams studded with thick-ended screws. The rooftop access was easy to find, a ladder screwed to the side of the building in the back, and so he climbed up and found a small trapdoor under the stingray's stubby tail. He unlatched it and it swung down; it almost hit him in the head. The room inside was small but he could crawl a few body lengths. In the middle he sat down and waited a few minutes, then got up and found the light switch, finally curling on the floor and using his arms as a makeshift pillow, he fell asleep.

*

He was beginning to amass a secondary store up in the stingray. Amanda didn't care too much about her job, and in the mornings she'd let Elias take whatever he wanted as long as he didn't cart off noticeable armloads of merchandise.

"Tell me what it's like to be a hobo," she commanded of him this morning. The way she said *hobo* sounded like she might have said *unicorn* or *rich*. She'd wrapped him up in a neat little package with a sparkling bow: to have a freedom like his meant life had promises yet unfulfilled.

"It's nothing special," he replied. He'd narrowed down his choice of shirt to a white one with a picture of a great white shark swimming in a badly water-colored ocean and a tan shirt that said *Just Wave* and showed a whale on a surfboard, balancing on the split end of his tail like it was legs. "Actually, it's kind of hard."

"What's hard is spending your summer working in your dad's stupid store."

Elias thought *stupid* was a word for people younger than them but didn't say anything.

"Can't wait to get out of here," she added.

"You could take the money in the cash register and run," he suggested, and the moment that idea escaped his mouth, he regretted it. The store grew very quiet and then Amanda laughed.

"Yeah, right," and then she switched gears saying, "get the whale shirt. The shark one has a janky collar. Well, all of them do, but the whale shirt not so bad."

Elias' stomach rumbled audibly, and he tried to cover up the sound by coughing.

"How do you eat?" she asked, leaning over the counter and sizing up his small body. "I mean, I know *how* you eat, but *what* do you eat?"

"Stuff," he said softly. "People leave stuff around."

"Aren't you worried about being arrested?"

He was, but he didn't want to admit it. His parents had picked a good town for vagrancy; the police didn't patrol much at night and even then they rarely got out of their cars, just drove down the streets and beach at low tide swinging the spotlight rather carelessly. "Not really," he said instead, and then, in an effort to impress her, "I know how to get around alone."

"Why'd you run away, anyway?"

He hadn't told her he'd run away. "I didn't like my parents." It hurt him to say this. It felt like he'd swallowed a tortilla chip the wrong way and it poked and scratched his throat. He folded the whale shirt slowly and clutched it to his chest.

"Lucky," she said. "I wish I were that brave. I bet it's not so easy to survive in LA either. Lots of people go there to get famous."

Elias felt he might cry and needed to get out of the store. "Isn't it time for you to open?"

"Yeah. Yeah." She came out from behind the counter and flipped the sign at the front door. "Water?"

Elias took the bottle without saying thanks and heard the door chime on his way out.

*

Hurricane became a word that flavored everyone's sentences. Noman was going to hit the east coast of Florida. Within a few days, the families with their plump children and the skinny beer-drinking college kids fled and left the locals to prepare. Elias was not so concerned for himself—he knew if he needed her to, Amanda would let him bunk down with her family. But he did find himself getting more worried about the crabs.

He watched from a bench on the sidewalk above the beach as the team of researchers from some university stalked around the perimeter of the sand castle safety zone. They had clipboards in their hands and wore dark sunglasses and caps or visors.

Elias stuck his hands in the pockets of the swimsuit he now wore as shorts and shuffled down the beach towards them. He saw that one of the castles had collapsed on its side and the moat was filling with sand. A crab blended in so well with the landscape that at first he didn't see it; then its whitish belly resolved into shape and he knew it was dead on its back.

"Hey," he said softly to a dark-bearded man in sandals, "what's going to happen to them?"

The man bent at the knees to inspect the dead crab and spoke to Elias like he was a child. "Hello son. You worried about them?"

Elias shook his head yes.

"Don't," the man said. His smile was full of impossibly white teeth.

They looked buried in his facial hair. "We're moving them today. They'll be okay."

Elias wanted to ask more questions, but the man stood up and yelled for someone else. A flash of a pincher appeared in the opening of a turret. Elias had seen people shaking their fists to the skies in old movies when they were angry. The motion reminded him of that.

There were pickup trucks parked on the street in the fire lane, their beds full of wood and plastic. Men and women nailed particle board over windows. Elias slipped into the ice cream store where the manager stood with his teenage employees, watching a flat screen TV. The newscaster said Noman was expected to make landfall that night and listed the names of towns that were evacuating. Elias didn't understand where they were on the coastal map streaked with red and orange, but the store owner said, "Whew! If we were any more north, you all wouldn't have jobs to come back to."

The employees didn't look overly delighted.

When Elias exited into the greying day, businesses were already closing and cars were lining up to get through the ill-planned stoplight at the boulevard's major intersection.

By the time he made it to the souvenir store, it too had closed. He cupped his hands against the window and breathed heavily onto the glass, but no one was inside.

*

His hands were on the ladder up the stingray when he remembered the fallen castle. What if, by some chance, there was a crab inside? Maybe the male had just died, and the female was scared and alone with her young clutched to her belly, hiding in the broken rooms and waiting for a prince to come.

Would it be worth it, he wondered, to check?

He climbed down onto the roof of the store, looking out over the awning, across the street, towards the beach. No beach umbrellas, snack carts. No towels. No beach balls. No bodies. The waves crested white closer to the sand, but in the distance where the water met dark sky, there was nothing but unremarkable expanse.

He wanted to go, to find out if the crabs had been removed. How they had been removed, how their castles had been preserved and taken to safety, if indeed that's what happened. But the sky began to drop water on him, and the wind plucked at his shorts, and Elias had never weathered a hurricane before; good sense prevailed, and it sent him up the ladder and into the stingray.

*

He left the light on. No one was in the streets to see him.

The bulb above him flickered periodically and finally went out for good. The streetlights outside failed too, trapping him in the musty darkness.

He thought he heard his mother's voice, and his father's, not words but the tones of their calling. He imagined they weren't his parents at all, but sirens singing him to his death. They were never his parents, these two who slipped in and out of scales. He shouldn't have told Amanda he never heard of selkies. He should have told her yes, he had, but that selkies were just creatures created in the minds of sirens seeking to throw humans off the correct path. He should have told her that he's figured it all out, that his "parents" had figured it out too: sirens cannot take care of human children, no matter how much they might want to.

He hunkered down and buried his head between his knees while the stingray groaned. He sweated inside the metal frame and the towels under him grew damp.

He tried to eat powdered donuts but his hands shook and his fingers crushed them into soft pieces that were lost in the darkness.

It sounded like he was in a tin can being pelted by nails. The sharpness pierced his ears and made the place behind his eyes hurt.

When it grew quiet, Elias' body was tired. He told himself he should have looked up hurricanes at the library.

*

The hatch under the stingray's tail swung open, revealing that water had pooled on the flat roof. It collected in puddles and for once Elias was glad he had no socks. They would have been soaked.

Outside it looked like someone had opened the largest bag of trash in the world and dumped it everywhere. Elias couldn't even identify what the trash was, just that there were bits of things on the sidewalks and the boards nailed over windows were splintered and glass was going to crunch underfoot and a lamppost had fallen through the window of the ice cream store and mud was splattered on doors and cement and the sludge made the grey look brown.

Business owners and people who hadn't left town were rolling slowly down streets and assessing the damage.

Amanda did not return. Elias waited for her to come to the store but hid when her father appeared to unlock and open it. When the police appeared a little while later, their radios crackling and Amanda's father pointing inside, Elias took off. He put his head down and slapped his flip flops along the sidewalk and to the beach. There were some people out, picking up what the storm had brought ashore. A man in Bermuda shorts waved around a metal detector and a loose dog jumped into the surf. One of the lifeguard towers had fallen over and a beach patrol 4x4 circled it, parked, and the man driving it got off and stared at it with hands on his hips.

Elias did his best to find the spot where the crabs should have been, but of course the sand castles were gone. The beach was wiped clean of signs and posters and dotted with dead fish and man-o-wars. He stepped on one of the creatures on accident, his foot slipping on its smooth head, and took a tumble into the sand.

His stomach rumbled but there was no food, and no Amanda, so Elias went to the only other place he could think of: the library.

He tried to act smooth, like he was just some vacation kid, and came in, nodding to the woman at the front desk. The place was virtually empty. He went to the bathroom and quickly bathed in the sink, drying himself off with paper towels. He passed the librarian's office on his way back towards the stacks and saw a tray with a few forlorn pastries, but he steered himself away from them.

Elias ended up in a beanbag chair in the children's balcony where he had a good view of the large clock in the lobby, and he passed as much time as he could reading some book about what every fifth-grader should know. He had not known about all the different types of clouds, or the reversal of seasons on either side of the equator. He had not known about linking verbs, though he saw from the examples that he used them often, and he had not known about personification, but his mother had used if often, explaining everything had a soul, even rocks and sea glass. He had known about glaciers, and Columbus, and decimal places, which made him feel a bit better about himself. But still, there was so much he would need to understand if he was going to be on his own.

At a quarter to five the woman at the front desk disappeared into the office. Elias came down from the balcony and took off his sandals, holding them in one hand and the book in the other.

There was a thick stack of newspapers on the counter near the scanning checkout machine. A photo collage in black and white showed the damage to the ice cream store, a palm tree buried in someone's roof, and a van, partially buried in sand on the beach.

Elias paused to look at the picture, but then he heard a toilet flush and took off through the door, the alarm beeping behind him because of the stolen book.

*

Elias had put his book aside and was scrounging for donut crumbs, careful to keep his body low so he couldn't be seen through the stingray's eyes, when there was a knock at the hatch. Before he could move, take a breath even, the hatch swung down and Amanda's head stuck up through the opening. The relief he felt might have been as great as seeing his parents appear, and before she could climb up into his small space he began crying and lunged at her, catching the girl below her breasts and heaving massive sobs into her chest.

"Elias, Elias, look it's okay. I'm okay." She didn't push him away but stood standing with half her body inside the stingray, raising her arms to stroke his dirty hair. For only a moment he thought that he wasn't glad she was alive, he was glad he wasn't alone. Then he heard another voice.

"Is he alright?"

Elias pulled himself away and wiped his eyes with his hands. Amanda crawled in and then her boyfriend's head appeared. "Hey little man," he said, pulling himself in and hunkering in the stingray; it was a tight fit with the three of them inside.

Elias couldn't say anything or else he knew he'd start crying again.

Amanda leaned forward and hugged him and she smelled like coconuts and suntan oil. "We're going," she whispered in his ear. He held on tighter and hid his face in her armpit.

"Don't leave me," he said, and she rubbed his back.

"We won't. We won't. Come on. Come out of here."

The boyfriend went down the ladder first and when Elias' legs wouldn't hold his own weight, the boyfriend climbed back up and told Elias to hang on around his neck. He put his hand out and Elias looked at the ground and took it.

Inside the souvenir store a thin layer of mud coated the floor. Most of it was dry, but Amanda's feet slipped on a wet spot hidden in the darkness behind the counter and she swore. "There's nothing here," she said and slammed the tiller shut.

"Isn't there a safe?" the boyfriend suggested.

She disappeared through a door into the back, leaving Elias and the boyfriend alone.

"You want anything in here?" he asked. "Like, a keepsake or something?"

Elias found himself unwilling to let go of the boyfriend's hand. He knew they'd be driving a long way, but he also knew how to make use of space. He led the boyfriend to the front of the store where he pointed to the inflatable palm tree.

"That's a good idea," the boyfriend agreed. "Take a bit of home with us." He grabbed the tree and put it under his arm.

"You can squeeze the air out," Elias told him.

"Nah, I think it's better like this."

The boyfriend helped Elias pack a beach bag with t-shirts and swim trunks and a sweatshirt. On top he put a travel kit kept for tourists who forgot necessary items: toothbrush, mini toothpaste, comb, band aids, deodorant. Elias saw their reflection in the mirrors of the makeshift dressing room. If he squinted, it looked like he was shopping with his father.

Amanda returned with a leather envelope. She held it up and waved it over her head.

In front of the store the boyfriend loaded Elias' bag and palm tree into the back of his van. "Hurry up, Chad," Amanda said, drumming her fingers on the door.

"Okay little man, pile in."

Elias climbed into the back and leaned his head against the palm tree.

They drove through town and he looked out the window at bungalow houses with plastic flamingos and wind chimes hanging from porches. His last thought before they got on the highway was of the crabs. If they were alive in plastic containers. If their castles stood intact. If the babies would let go of their mothers and find their way to the ocean. If there were any left at all.

A CARNIVAL, IN PIECES

I.   Parceled Puzzle

"This Carnival is full of secrets," the soda-bottle man chimes at the entrance, townspeople passing under the paint-stripped sign, all wide-eyed with snowy faces and wind-blown hair. The soda-bottle man hands each patron a cardboard scrap with the numbers one through five written in a shaky script, and he tells them, "a grand prize awaits for those who can discover what the Carnival seeks to keep hidden." He offers stubby pencils, some not much more than a piece of lead sticking out from the eraser. Soon the ground is littered with what he's tried to give away. In between the waves of curious visitors, he gathers what has been tossed down—the cardboard and the pencils—and waits to redistribute them.

*

The bulbs pulsate a message: lights wink on and off, slow and fast, visual Morse code. The message is carried down the string of lights, each one echoing the last. If lights could scream, the carnival-goers would be deaf. One of the bulbs is whining and when it begins its coded message, it pops, showering the lady who carries a stuffed narwhal with bits of glass. The woman's sisters laugh. She scowls.

The fortune-telling girl lazes in a hanging chair outside her tent, feet tapping and pushing against the pole supporting her sign. She smiles at the woman and her sisters, but they are not interested in knowing the future.

"Can you imagine," the woman says, brushing shards off her furry creature and passing by the fortune-telling girl, "anything worse than knowing what's coming?"

Her sisters do not hear what she says; they are pointing to the advert of the Fully Tattooed Man.

The fortune-telling girl, however, hears what the woman says and does not agree. Since she knows the future, has become used to what will happen, it doesn't seem too awful. In fact, it has become mundane. So boring and predictable are the years to come that the fortune-telling girl has shifted all her attention to *now* instead of *when*. While the fortune-telling girl sees new jobs and car wrecks, marriages and stillbirths, financial collapse and the end of civilization, these are just *things*, events to occur. To create some fun for herself—to escape the grand cycle of civilization—she likes to narrate the lives of the other carnival workers and their customers, because the future is always certain, but the present, ah, that is another story.

Ajax skirts the big top, its creaky ball lights hum-drumming and flickery. What terrible light to poke his brain with reminders of before this place. Ajax thinks of rock piles and cold stone and of an empty cabin that used to be home.

This boy, Ajax, is sweeping up glass, ignoring the jeers from inside the tent, trying to avert his eyes from the gaps in the canvas walls. The big top's poster reads "complimentary nudity" because it is past 9pm: adults only, save the children who work here. The pretzel carts have been rolled away, the elephant ear stand now transformed into a corndog stand. Only phallic foods are served once the sun goes down.

The broken glass sparkles in the blinking lights and Ajax scans the dirt for any pieces he might have missed. When he looks up, he sees the fortune-telling girl across the lane, swinging in her hanging chair, looking back at him. When he walks to the trash can, she follows. When he puts away the broom and dustpan, she is behind him. When he goes to the supply cart to get his mason jar, she is sticking close to shadows, humming in the dark.

"Would you stop it?" Ajax says to no one he can see. "I have work to do."

His tummy all grumbles and bubbles. He walks on, head down, swinging his net with careless abandon. Fireflies are buzzy and watery. They appear here, there, here, there. He scoops them up with his trickery wrist, snapping the fabric in time to the organ music cranked by the grinder, his parrot screaming along.

When Ajax turns out his prize under the gas lamp, tumbling forth bugs from the mason jar his father used to keep in his lunchbox, Ajax sees a rather sad assortment. Nine fireflies, twelve mosquitoes, two June bugs, and something he does not recognize, a large bug brown and green, its antennae blindly radaring. Luckily, the Ferris wheel doesn't eat much.

*

The Ferris wheel is acting up and sometimes won't let passengers out of their cages. The carnival master and the boy as strong as an ox have to come with a crowbar and make a great show of huffy-puffy laboring until the Ferris wheel at last tires its chops and relents with a sigh. The carnival master and the boy as strong as an ox bow, and the carnival master says something like, "What a show! What a show! I really thought they wouldn't make it out." None the wiser, the happy family emerges, slobbery and made of stupid grins, to receive their hasty prize: coupons for a free sugar cone for surviving "the trap".

Ajax is thinking about how sullen the Ferris wheel is, how difficult it is to care for, and is still wondering after all these months why he is the primary worker assigned to it. He wastes hours collecting bugs and his fingers are constantly wrinkled with the Ferris wheel's goo. Most of all he hates its smell: like damp earth, like stagnant water, like flesh just beginning to rot. He has complained to the carnival master about all this—demonstrated his proficiency at troubleshooting the ball bearings on the tilt-a-wheel, shown how to align the wonky wheels on the dragon coaster, even timed himself in mopping up puke that cascades over the side of the pirate boat—but to no avail.

As Ajax leaves the carnival proper and crosses into the high grass of the nearest field, he shakes the mason jar, throwing the bugs into the glass walls, knocking them to the bottom where all legs up, they make the saddest of dance parties. The Ferris wheel waits, standing black against the sky, its cages squeaking and turning in delight to Ajax's footfalls.

II. The Ferris Wheel

After a few hours of sleep Ajax climbs down from his bunk on the big bus, careful not to wake Lucinda, the woman who sleeps below him and who sells young bunnies out of an old Victorian baby buggy. Ajax gets up before everyone else to collect more bugs—always bugs—for the Ferris wheel's breakfast.

He searches the wheel wells of the bus for spiders. Turns over rocks to find roly-polies and centipedes. Twirls in the silent, empty lanes between tents with a net in his hand, collecting anything airborne, even butterflies.

In the field, the Ferris wheel's pods are beginning to tilt towards the sky, beginning to gape their weird mouths, the soft eyelashes of their non-lips parting to become lazy bars. Ajax thinks the pods of the Ferris wheel look like funhouse watermelons, vibrant green on the outside, pinkish-red inside. Ajax thinks it looks kind of like a regular Ferris wheel, a non-monstrous one, if he squints and pretends it is metal *painted* green. From its central stalk the buds stick out in a circular pattern, some closer to the bottom, some closer to the top, a circle. All the pods equidistant from the bottom, but their stems taking turns lengthening and coiling, a rotation that makes the movement more mechanical and less threatening.

"C'mon," he says, tickling the lining of the lowest pod's mouth. "Open up."

The bud begins to yawn, revealing the space inside: a light wood church pew scavenged from a defunct tent ministry somewhere in the bible belt. Ajax steps inside, the sunlight streaming in behind him, casting patches of neon, blood-colored fibers in too-bright light.

He picks the trash out of the Ferris wheel: butter-soiled popcorn containers and wax-lined cups. Spare bits of change fallen out of pockets (which he pockets) and dried leaves and twigs. Torn in half tickets and scraps of cardboard no one has put their answers on.

The fourth pod is coming down and the sun is coming up. It opens its cavity and Ajax lets loose a string of words previously forbidden to him. Inside is a partially digested body.

III. (dis)Enchantment

The master is groany and full of clouds. He exhales them in longish puffs; they swirl into the shapes Ajax sees in the sky: crippled dogs, lattice-work earrings, plastic soldiers, windmills, beer bottles. Outside his tent the touristas wipe snooty noses and their words droop, falling out of their mouths like watery oatmeal. They are tired and full of amusement and musing. Silly cows going back to their pastures with broken boxes of caramel corn, fingertips sweet and stickery.

The fortune-telling girl never sleeps, but this is not one of the carnival's secrets. It should be, the fortune-telling girl thinks, because there is no way any visitor could ever guess it.

She is looking through the foggy window of the carnival master's bus. She is not old enough to see what's taking place inside, but what are eyes when one has all the knowledge of how lives will end? How families will be torn apart? How generations of children will be tainted by the actions of one man two hundred years ago?

Inside, Bathsheba is dancing.

Ah tasty Bathsheba. Honeyed milk and almond eyes. Tastes like cinnamon rolls and smells like swamp.

The carnival master's belly quivers in tune with the calliope. The belly dancers are drunk on wine and make-believe. Their breasts sway and jiggle. When Bathsheba drops a scarf, the carnival master claims it with a fat, unshod toe.

Dear sweetum, won't you ever learn?

The fortune-telling girl once read Bathsheba's future. "This is bullshit," (s)he proclaimed when it was over and done, but both of them knew the truth. Simply refusing to acknowledge does not a reality make.

Slippery seal. Fat, shiny, thick-legged barker. Look at you with your button eyes and whiskers, always gobbling up the yummiest fish. Squishy squishy sad and slippery.

Bathsheba winks at the carnival master but does not bend down to retrieve the scarf. A pity that is. It is a favorite, woven silk of peach and blue, hand-stitched with tiny golden chickens. (S)he remembers the fortune that made her so angry. It's been whittled down from a tree to a toothpick. (S)he keeps it hidden in her hair, just in case.

You just wait, bulbous quivery.

The carnival master wiggles his fingers, eager to touch, eager to feel wanted.

Ajax sees the fortune-telling girl, standing on a crate and peering through the window, and makes a wide berth around her, knocking on the side of the bus and climbing the rickety steps up into it.

When the carnival master opens the door, he does so as if what's happening inside is private. The folding metal door hisses and the master puts his hand up to stop from revealing all.

"Ajax," he says.

"We have a problem with Ferris," Ajax tells him.

"Which is?"

"I think it ate a guest."

*

"Well, this probably isn't good." The carnival master stands in his smoking jacket and unicorn slippers and looks inside the pod.

"It can't be too bad, right?" Alice asks. "No one's come asking questions yet." She's still in her bird costume. Ajax begins to wonder if she ever takes it off, or if she believes she actually is a peacock, refusing to look at her own naked, human body even hours before the shows start.

"Doesn't mean they won't," signs Hans. He's been brought over from his post in the canteen because the boy as strong as an ox is missing an action and Hans is the next most powerful person around.

Then, too quick for Ajax to follow, Hans' fingers curl and his hands flash, a comment only for the carnival master to know.

"Did you check him for ID?" the carnival master asks Ajax, to which he shakes his head no. "Well, go on then."

The Ferris wheel has been patient. It hasn't moved since Ajax first spotted the worn trousers, and it hasn't even creaked one complaint. But despite the Ferris wheel's docility, Ajax doesn't want to step inside.

Seeing the hesitation, Hans makes a move forward to do this dirty work for the boy, but the Ferris wheel begins to slowly close its mouth-eye and Ajax sighs.

"Sorry," Hans signs. "It only really likes you."

Ajax goes to the Ferris wheel's pod and looks inside. The body is covered in thick strands of shiny mucous. When he steps in, the soft skin of the wheel's body is like walking on jello. He puts a hand against the wall to steady himself while he examines the body.

It seems cemented to the pew, but Ajax manages to heft his own weight and push it aside enough to finger the man's pockets, which do produce a wallet. A dry one.

Ajax passes this out and then wipes his hands on his pants. The viscous fluid smells like chlorophyll.

"Thomas Smith," the carnival master laughs, doubling over and slapping his knee. "This can't be his real name!"

Hans signs and then the carnival master adds, "He's not a *spy*. First, a spy would have a less spy-like name. Secondly, there is no reason for a spy to be carousing around our carnival."

Hans signs again.

"Yes," the carnival master draws out, "it is *possible* that you've been pursued all the way from Europe, but I should remind you that war is long over and you never really were anyone important."

Hans looks hurt.

"I'm not saying you're not an important person, in general," the carnival master amends, "simply that you weren't important to the Nazis." He turns to Ajax. "You might as well come out from there. Drag that body out here for Hans."

Ajax isn't sure how he is supposed to manage this, but he begins with grabbing the body's foot, pulling it off the pew, and sludging it along the pod's floor towards daylight.

"Oh shit," Alice says, "I forgot to give the wake-up call."

IV. A Coincidence of Catastrophe

Here our hero, swift Ajax alight with a ladder. Rickety splittery he better be careful. Gods do not like men who climb too high.

Salt is stinging Ajax's eyes, his head down and turned to the side, forced by the weight of the ladder on his back. In his mouth he gently holds the metal tip of a bulb. He prays he does not trip or run his ladder into anything.

In the big top the acrobats are drunk and practicing. Through the slits in the fabric siding, Ajax can see them in their skin-tight leotards, sweat under their armpits and at their crotches. They are cartwheeling and handstanding, tumbling and leaping. From the ceiling a man hangs from a swaying bar, frog-legged and yelling. A jug is tossed up to him and he uncorks it, filling his upside-down mouth and spilling it all over. Below him a woman on a unicycle tries to keep her balance, head thrown back, while attempting to catch the wine falling from above.

At the top of the ladder Ajax realizes he cannot extract the broken glass so easily. The bulb has left jagged pieces of itself sticking out of the metal cap. He removes his shirt and wraps it around his hand to protect it. Bathsheba whistles at him.

With the new bulb in place, Ajax can see the filament glowing and darkening. Staring directly at it, he also notices a pattern.

Clever imp. Eyes are *made for seeing I've always heard. What secretive do you spy? What message flash then die?*

Ajax knows the code—*SOS*—because his own hands had

fashioned it into being all those years ago, covering the lamp, uncovering it, desperately hoping someone would walk by and see the light from the tunnel. His father had tapped the rhythm onto Ajax's thigh, his own legs pinned beneath rocks, while Ajax's hand moved towards and away from the glass, the pattern repeating long after his father's hand stopped moving.

*

Does not know it, boy is romping the wrong way.

Ajax is playing keep away with the fish-eyed twins. Melinda has stolen her sister's sunglasses and is tossing them over Iris' head at him. *Keep away, keep away.* Her voice is something masquerading as soft grass.

"I can't see," Iris complains. The fish-eye twins have eyes too large for their heads. Their pupils are always dilated big and black and they have to wear specialty sunglasses with extra-large frames to protect them in the daylight. Iris' eyes are closed. Her hands are outstretched.

She's almost pretty now he thinks. Her skin flaps closed, she's almost a girl. Not too quick young man, you're skippiting into a pit.

Ajax catches the glasses and runs. He ducks around a corner and hides behind the ice cream cart. The alligator man and the bald woman are talking.

The bald woman sounds like a songbird but looks like a bull.

"No one saw it. At least no one will admit it," Ajax hears the bald woman say. He can smell the sunscreen coming from her head. It smells like sweet coconuts.

"Then how do you *know*," the alligator man asks.

"Because in the morning they found a body. Inside."

"Ajax!" Iris is yelling and close by the organ grinder's monkey starts screeching.

"A mouse in the kitchen?" the man says, nodding towards the twins and the monkey.

Ajax can hear the alligator man and the bald woman retreating, quieter footsteps and voices.

He feels a tug on his hand, and the fortune-telling girl is trying to take Iris' glasses from him.

"Stop it," he hisses, shaking her off, standing up, taking a step back. He wants to tell the fortune-telling girl to go away. He wants to call her a creepy old bat and run away from her, but he doesn't want to look like a wimp.

"Mean tricks for mean boys," she whispers to him.

"I'm not mean," he whispers back. Iris is getting closer. He can hear Alice laughing.

"The dark is not a nice place to be, is it?"

And she's right. Ajax can remember a terrible dark he'd rather not experience again.

All the gears aturning, all the cheer a'burning.

Ajax looks at Iris stumbling around. He watches her trip and fall. There is donkey poop on her knees, and she is brushing it off, thinking it mud.

"Here," he says, placing the sunglasses on her face.

She reaches to adjust them but her hands stink and he adds, "better let me do this. You're covered in shit."

Iris frowns when she can see what's happened to her.

Ajax wonders what he looks like to a fish-eyed girl. A buzzing bug or a blunt-end bat.

"Damnit Ajax," Iris says.

Boil, boil, toil and trouble.

"Stop pouting," Ajax tells her. "You're too young to look so ugly."

V.   Overlord

The carnival has rented a collection of connected fields from a man with too much land and nothing to do. Rattal Weaver and the carnival master look like lumpy mirror twins of each other, and now their voices carry through the grass and reach the ears of Ajax, who understands that they will be leaving sooner rather than later and that yes, the carnival master did *imply* two weeks but the crowds just weren't what they needed to be to warrant a longer settle-down.

Ajax can hear them better than he can see them. He is taking his shift guarding the Ferris wheel. It is off-limits, the carnival master's decree, from most employees and all carnival patrons until they can figure out what is going on with it.

The Ferris wheel is drooping, its pods turned down like lily of the valley. This new posture has occurred slowly over the course of the day while Ajax's back is pressed against its stalk. He's been so caught up in *Doctor Futurity*, a paperback someone left on a stray crate, that he hasn't paid any attention to what is going on behind and above him.

"Impossible!" Weaver's voice is so shrill Ajax winces. "The whole damn town is out here every night!"

Ajax thinks he can make out the carnival master shrugging.

Ajax knows they need to get away. It could be days, or months, or years before the remains of the man-who-is-not-a-spy are found, but better they be long gone no matter how much time has passed.

Weaver says something Ajax cannot hear and is wagging his finger in the carnival master's face. Then, huffing and crunching his hat in one hand, Weaver storms off, pushing past Hans who is coming to relieve Ajax of his duty.

Hans signs "what's wrong with Ferris?" and Ajax turns around.

The sun is blocked by one of the limp pods, its mouth sagging open, the pew inside, for some reason, unanchored and resting against the eyelash teeth that keep it from crashing out on the ground.

"I don't know," Ajax says. "Maybe it's sick."

Inside, he is hopeful this means he can become something other than the bug-boy.

*

"Dear God. They're like buzzards." Bathsheba sits next to Ajax, who has brought water, the two of them huddling in the darkness, the she-man's orange tipped cigarette glowing, and dying, bright, then smoldering.

The townsfolk are gluttons, devouring candied orange rinds and chili-pepper popcorn, fried ice cream, and salted pickles the size of small logs.

"I think buzzards eat road kill," Ajax says. He can hear the men in the tent behind them, impatient for the show to start.

"Hawks then, whatever," Bathsheba remarks.

They do kind of look like ugly birds, Ajax thinks. Dressed to impress plumage, their heads craned forward, necks bent, snapping at their food.

"Oh, look, I bet that's her!" Bathsheba exhales smoke rings, nodding to the woman in the green knee-length skirt whom all the carnival workers are talking about. She has her little scrap of cardboard in one hand, stubby pencil in the other, looking up at the blinking lights.

Tonight's rumors started with Nellie who saw that the woman in the green knee-length skirt had at least one correct answer thus far.

And then Boris the Merman had bent over to flirt with the woman in the green knee-length skirt a bit during his show and saw the card, in her lap this time, with a second correct answer.

Now all the workers were keeping tabs on her, waiting to see if someone would finally win, and if so, what the grand prize was going to be.

The fish-eyed twins are trailing the woman, whispering to each other.

"I better get going," he says. "It's dinner time."

*

The Ferris wheel is uninterested in dinner. It has no desire to slime bugs, or brush its bristle teeth against moth wings. Ajax can see that its wetness has dulled, the inside of its pods matte and cracking.

The carnival master is arguing with a couple who claims they've come only to ride the Ferris wheel, but now find it out of commission; they want their entrance cost refunded.

"But you enjoyed the snake charmer, yes?" the carnival master counters. "And look at that sweet, stuffed cow you've got. Beat the guess the weight game, did you?" He only gives back half their money, and they stand, hesitant to leave, peering through the darkness at Ajax and the Ferris wheel.

Hans arrives to relieve the boy, who sits and twists long stalks of grass into braids. Hans signs about the woman in the green knee-length skirt, and how she has one secret left. "But she's noticed all our skulking," he adds, "and so we need to back off."

Ferris is looking even worse, sickly in the glow of artificial lights, its central stalk now seeming to slag.

"Did it eat?" Hans signs.

"I tried." Ajax gets up and brushes dirt off his butt. He reaches down to collect his mason jar and leads Hans over to the pod resting its great weight on the ground. "Come on big boy," Ajax says, tickling the whiskery fuzz of its mouth. "Time to eat."

Ferris does not open up.

"Tell it that if it does not eat it will not get better," Hans signs.

"If you don't eat, you're not going to get better. Come on."

No prodding, rubbing, or slapping will do. The Ferris wheel refuses to cooperate.

Ajax slides his hands into the soft flesh of the pod's mouth and begins pulling and pushing. "You. Are. Going. To. Eat. Dinner," he says.

Then he feels something rend, or give loose. He isn't sure. The pod relaxes and the bottom half falls open, falls off, the loud snap of something dry ripping.

VI. Too Blurry to Discern

Gloomy doomy under the moonie.

The fortune-telling girl watches Ajax. Too many unhappy customers tonight, including one woman who stood outside the tent after an especially auspicious telling, warning others that the girl was a sham. A hack. A liar and a cheat.

The fortune-telling girl has just come from the carnival master's bus where the man is gathering news of the woman in the green knee-length skirt like it is gold. His face was red and huffing when he told the fortune-telling girl what she must do.

Ajax and the mute man are walking circles around the Ferris wheel, Ajax with the jar in his hands and the mute man scratching his head.

The fortune-telling girl kicks up dirt with her boots. She walks with a purpose. She ignores the sly smile of the balloon-twister, his metal pole dangling with rubber birds, dogs. She whistles along with the guitar played by the alligator man. The lights along the tents blink and dull; the fortune-telling girl snaps her fingers in time with the message being carried down the line.

She finds the woman in the green knee-length skirt in front of the ring toss; the woman's boyfriend is loudly lamenting his frustration. The woman is only half paying attention to the man who throws clinking rings against glass bottles. Her eyes are on the lip of the tent, watching those lights the fortune-telling girl knows so well.

"Have you figured it out yet?" the fortune-telling girl asks.

"I think so," the woman replies, her eyes not leaving the lights.

"Then why don't you write it down?"

The man with the woman in the green knee-length skirt cheers for himself. He has anchored one ring.

"Should I?" the woman asks, turning to look at the girl by her side.

The girl shrugs.

The woman in the green knee-length skirt sighs. "I don't know," she says more to herself than the fortune-telling girl. She looks at her man, and her eyes are shining with wetness.

The fortune-telling girl eases the cardboard scrap from the woman's hand and then says, "Come, I have something to tell you."

*

The carnival master stands with his legs far apart and his hands on his ample hips. Bathsheba is to one side, Alice to the other. "Well, shit," he says. "It was good while it lasted."

The Ferris wheel is emitting an odor and the part of its pod that lays on the ground is attracting flies, even at night, when flies seem to sleep.

"What do we do?" Ajax asks. He still holds the mason jar.

"We don't do anything," the carnival master says.

"You want to leave it?" Hans signs.

"No point in dragging it along with us."

Ajax is not sure how he feels about this statement. He never did like the Ferris wheel much, but knowing it will be abandoned to this field while it withers makes his hands shake a bit.

"Whelp. That's that." The carnival master claps his hands once and walks off.

"What do you think is wrong with it?" Alice asks.

"The same thing that's wrong with this whole damn carnival," Bathsheba says, wrinkling her nose.

Ajax strains his eyes and sees a fracture in the stalk of another pod, the moonlight spilling through the gap that should not be there.

"It liked you," Hands signs, and then puts a big hand on Ajax's shoulder.

Alice moves to sit on the church pew that has fallen from inside the pod. "Should we say something? Memorial service?"

"You were an okay Ferris wheel," Bathsheba replies. "You would have been better if you didn't try to eat people."

Across the field, the music from the carnival changes. The calliope to drums, the booms of stretched skin beat with mallets.

"It's nine," Bathsheba says. "I got to get ready." (S)he yawns and rubs her face. "Oh. And we pack up in the morning."

*

Ajax is in the fields with his net, so he does not know that the woman in the green knee-length skirt has collected her boyfriend and stormed out of the carnival, her prize unclaimed. He does not know that everyone is whispering about her—no, not the woman in the green knee-length skirt—but the fortune-telling girl, who was the last person to say anything to the woman.

The fortune-telling girl knows the future. All of it.

What she does not let anyone know is that the future is immense and branches like the roots of a tree. The woman in the green knee-length skirt will lose the tip of her left pointer finger if she moves into the house on Goliad street. She will become the head of a boarding school for unwanted children if she plays the lottery on Tuesday, April 7th, and wins more money than she knows what to do with. If the woman in the green knee-length skirt vacations in Orlando the summer of her thirty-third year, she will become so ill from food poisoning that she will lose twenty pounds and when she emerges from the hospital, she will hear her husband say, *you look really good*, and this will stay with her through the next fifteen years of her life until she starves herself into a grave.

The fortune-telling girl sees all possible futures, and because she knows the paths, she can sometimes direct which ending will come to fruition simply by vocalizing some fortunes and muzzling others.

When her customers leave, shaking fists and crying and cursing her, they do not understand that what she says is for the best, and that sometimes, tragedy must be weathered in order to reach happiness.

Ajax is in the field twirling under the moon, his net missing all the lightning bugs flashing the Morse code of the carnival. He is looking up at the sky and thinking that the stars are all wrong, that he has traveled too far from home and that the constellations that spin in his vision are nothing like the names his father once called out when Ajax explained their positions in the sky while his father was pinned by the boulder, both of them waiting for help, Ajax's hand covering and uncovering the lamp that was running out of fuel.

When Ajax falls to the ground, dizzy with memory and sick to his stomach with phantom liquor—the mason jar forgotten in the grass, the beetles crawling over the lip, disappearing in long stems—he thinks the sirens he hears are help coming for his father.

"We're here!" he calls, closing his eyes.

And then his hand is held, and the fingers are the touch he's been longing to feel: proof that not all is lost on this dark night.

"It will be alright," the fortune-telling girl says, sitting beside Ajax and watching the bugs blink.

She wants to tell him that she's saved them all, and that the woman in the green knee-length skirt has saved them too, chosen the right path through all possible futures to see the carnival master in handcuffs, Bathsheba screaming and throwing a bottle at police officers, Hans trying to quiet her, Alice squawking in surprise when, asleep on the church pew in the rotting half of the Ferris wheel's maw, the beast lowers a pod around her and closes its lash-teeth firmly.

MAMMOTH MOOR

My father called this hotel The New Lion because the ghost of Saint Andrew told him to. I've never seen the saint, but my friends tell me they have. All of them—the rats, the spiders, the lizards, the roaches, the cats, the mice, and the bats (but never the moths because I've stopped inviting them to dinner since they tend to try to eat the runners and linens)—have reported him, the closest thing I have left to my father, some battle-granting sage floating the halls in a brown cowl, chanting passages from the *Book of Hours*. Perhaps I have not seen him yet because I've never been about to lose a battle; that's when my father saw him for the first time, though he rarely talked about it: the day we lost our court case and fled Scotland for South America.

My father also called this place New Moor even though it looks nothing like the village we came from. I know he missed the grey-washed sky, the deep browns and greens, the bleating of roaming sheep, the sound of bells in the morning, the coolness of our low stone house, the softness of Scotland. We arrived here with closely guarded suitcases, money hidden also in the folds of our shirts and pants, and bought the hotel. My father tried to make it like home. He hung small Scottish flags in our bedrooms and when guests were eating fried plantains and rice he made us porridge and "new" kippers. But in the end this place was too different, so textiles and decoration and traditional food gave way to the jungle with its heaviness and violent green leaves and Scotland became more memory than place.

He needed to feel less uprooted and because he was not good with Spanish, he always named things New _____, and this was a great source of amusement for our guests who resorted to hand gestures and badly drawn pictures on hotel stationery to communicate their needs. But this place is not New Moor. And there are no lions. This is a tropical, forested mountain, and this hotel is on a cliff above a river that is now brown and sends up foul smells. Our guests stopped coming when the river became polluted, a few months before my father fell ill. Now I fill the rooms with birds that eat the sick fish below and I try to make them comfortable as they die. Each day I climb down the stairs carved out of the cliff face, down to the river, and collect the fallen birds.

I try to maintain the hotel; however, I am not even a man and it's a fair amount of work. Four stories tall, Baroque Spanish, the roofing tiles now bound with green algae, it overlooks the waterfall that is part of this river. Now the waterfall and river are drying up, both a blessing and a curse.

*

I am preparing to reopen the hotel. It may not be as scenic without the water, but I refuse to let this place be a wasteland. In the morning and evening the mists come and the hotel looks like it is floating in the clouds. Tonight I scavenge the pantry once full of aluminum and brightly colored labels and my friends and I are eating tinned carrots and green beans, some hard cheese, and fresh bananas. I ring the dinner bells and they come from all over the hotel, attuned to the brass choir. They have no manners. I try to tell them to sit in their chairs and to say *please* and *thank you* but they talk with their mouths full, swarm the table. I preside over them like a hopeless school master. I don't know if they'll ever learn.

The balcony doors are open and the night air is cool. Moths sit on the railing, their wings coated with dew. The sun is beginning to set. The jungle is becoming quieter. Soon we will all prepare to sleep. The spiders will fold into shadowed corners and the lizards will drape themselves over the backs of chairs. The mice will find their nests of frayed thread and the beetles their dark homes between pages of swollen books. I dread this time, when I am alone in the darkness. Some nights the hotel is swallowed by it, thick and humid. Those nights feel like the night my father died. Outside the hotel, even the monkeys are quiet, clasped to branches or nestled in the crooks of trees. When I draw water from the well, I see that the bucket is becoming slick with algae again. I hum gently to myself while I work in the dark.

Before I retire to my own room, I check on the bird. There were ducks in the green room until two days ago, but now there is only the egret in the blue. It takes five trips up the stairs to fill the bathtub with water I've drawn. I put the bird into it, have to hold it up, its webbed feet trying to find a rhythm in the water. It seems to perk up when I do this. But then it becomes exhausted, its already deteriorating body beginning to fail, and I take it back to its bed where I feed it shredded fish I've caught from what's left of the river.

After this, I make my rounds: four levels of the hotel. All except for the servants' quarters. I carry my father's rifle in the case of intruders, although I've never seen anyone. Really, I am looking for Saint Andrew, but I can't admit this to my friends. I think they would make fun of me.

"Good night, Good night!" The crickets chirp back in song, and I call out to them that they're always invited to eat with us. I have not told my friends that our food supply is running out. I am afraid they will mutiny, or worse, leave.

*

On nights like this, when the fog billows in the river valley, I dream of my father and also of the mother I never knew. In these dreams we are in a bunker on the steam ship from Scotland to South America. My father is bent down to look under his bunk—he's hidden something there and it's obscured by his wide back. He looks like a giant fidgeting with children's toys. He is rearranging something—I see his shoulder blades working under his shirt, see the sweat matting down his red hair, damp at his neckline. He speaks softly and laughs when I ask him what he's doing. It's like I'm not there at all. He never responds.

When he gets up, closing the door behind him, I scurry across the room and suddenly the bunk is massive. I am miniature and can see every crumbling bit of hard bread on the floor like large rocks, the dust and dirt embedded in the planks like railroad tracks.

Under the bed is a birdcage, as large as a mansion. It looks Victorian, painted white with a domed top, like a church made out of bars. Inside it is lit with white lamps and looks like the cottage we've been forced to abandon. I put my hands against the metal and look inside. There is my mother, and she wears a brown wool robe, loose and wide in the sleeves. She is sitting at our table; she is resting her elbows on it and gesturing with open hands to a man across from her.

I know he is Saint Andrew, but he is made of bone and his fingers break off. They become slim gold bars like the ones my father hid under our clothes in the suitcases, and my mother takes them up in her hands. She grips them so hard her hands are white and shine like the lamps around them. Saint Andrew tells her, "Take them to the end of the earth where they'll be safe," and she nods her head.

*

When the sun comes up, the monkeys come out. I hear them screaming in the jungle. And this is all I hear. The sound of the water hitting the pool in the bottom of the gorge is gone. I get up and look out the window. I need to clean them badly but have run out of window cleaner, lemons, and vinegar. There is no waterfall.

I run down the stairs. The carpeting has come loose and I must find a way to tack it down before the hotel reopens. When I enter the dining room, I see that my friends have not cleaned up, again. In fact, they've left the balcony doors open and clearly the moths have gotten in. The seats are looking more threadbare.

Where the waterfall used to be, now there is only river stone, the cliff behind it smooth and concave like a spoon. When I look over the edge of the stone railing, there is only rock and mud. The fish have already died, I suspect.

Without any fish, my bird will starve. The stairs lead down to the bank and I take them two at a time. Some of the stairs are slick and I must remember to scrub them down. At the bottom, I search the drying river bed, feet sinking. Thank goodness I have no more shoes or they would be ruined. But this is a small victory because all the fish are still. I pick each up, assessing the time of its death. It's hard to tell how long they've been gone, and I collect a few just in case.

There is also something else here. White rods sticking up out of the mud. I lean over to inspect them, feet plopping and sticking. Each is different, white and brown, some broken and hollow. I do not know what they are so I leave them to take care of the bird.

In the blue room, the egret refuses to eat. I think it knows the fish aren't fresh and it turns its head away from me, lays it on the pillow. Its eyes are slits now and it's already beginning to flatten. It will be gone by the end of the day. I say a prayer for it, call to Saint Andrew to keep it company. I cannot sit in these rooms and wait for death.

*

The fog has burned off by the time I am done with breakfast, black beans and oatmeal, and I get to work cleaning the front of the hotel. My father once told me that ivy isn't nearly as beautiful as it looks. While romantic and curling, it sends out tendrils into mortar and brick, silently destroying over the years. The building is covered in ivy and I need to pull it all down.

My hands are red and raw by afternoon. The ivy is stronger than it looks. I draw water from the well to scrub the front steps, but the image of the white rods in the river bed keeps coming back to me. What could they possibly be? Not metal of course, and not plaster. Perhaps bone. Perhaps they're the leftovers of some great beast. I begin to construct its story: centuries ago the river was much larger. The beast was trying to cross it when it got stuck in the mud, just like me. It was too big to combat the vacuum its attempt to break free created, and it died there, leaving bones for me to find. This is enough to convince me I need to take another look, but before I walk down to the river bed I check on the egret. It is almost dead; I can't even see its chest moving. The sheets have rumpled its feathers and one wing is thrust out like a fan.

The river bed looks terribly dry already, though the clay surface breaks under foot to reveal the treachery I only just managed to escape earlier. While some of the rods are lodged between rocks, others are not, and it's not until I dig into the stinking mud and pull one free that I realize it *is* a bone. A giant bone. I fall backwards in disbelief and look around. I count seventeen, six of which, I think, are part of a massive ribcage opening to the sky. It might be a dinosaur. Nothing I know of is this large, except for an elephant, and there are none of those around here. A fish is impaled on the broken edge of one of the bones, the inside a honeycomb of dried marrow and dirt.

Without the waterfall, the only attraction I have is the mist. Perhaps a dinosaur would also entice the guests back. I pick up the bone I've uncovered, straining because it's heavier than I thought it would be. It is five feet long, as tall as I am, and it weighs about thirty pounds. It's tough going up the stairs. I have to move between bear-hugging the bone and lifting it up each step or carrying it across my shoulders. Neither is comfortable. By the time I drag it through the hotel and out front to clean it off, I think I've figured out what it is: a leg bone. I remember a skeleton chart from my old science class. This bone has two rounded bulbs on one side, stone-like onions that should fit into the pelvis.

I wait for it to dry in the sun while the monkeys across the dirt road drop down vines and branches, hanging low and shouting at me. I've never been able to understand what they say. When I was first alone and desperate for company I used to walk to the tree line and call out to them, invite them to dinner, but instead of accepting my invitation they threw down anything they could find, pelting my head and shoulders with fruit and flowers and even the eggs of birds who'd left their nests unattended. They're harsh, primal beasts. Sometimes I see them fighting, pulling at each other's fur and limbs. Once I even saw one smash another's head in with a rock.

Their white faces appear as flashes amongst the leaves. A thud hits the ground and a green papaya rolls towards me. I doubt it's a gesture of friendship.

When the bone is dry, I take it into the lobby. I see how I'll need to hang rope, or ivy, from the beams to string it up. I think it will be a good addition. The white and green-veined marble floors contrast with it nicely, and I hope it will all fit. This room is twenty feet high, and still may not be large enough.

*

At dinner I tell the spiders about the bone because the other animals are gluttonous and frenzied eaters—concerned with food, not me—but the spiders are at least half interested, though they are busy searching the webs they've strung up between dusty glasses and old cans for flies and other small flying bugs.

"No, really," I say when Martha pauses to listen to me. Her legs bob up and down on her silk, sewing machine needles testing weight. "I think the whole thing must be down there. I guess the pool at the bottom of the waterfall kept them in place instead of washing them down the stream. It's about ten feet deep by the way. I know you've always wondered."

I cannot determine where her eyes are; she is too small. But I think she's looking at me. She whispers something that I have to strain to hear.

"Can you repeat that?" I ask.

"A cave, a cave," she whispers. "It smells like chemicals and white. My heart is in my abdomen and I keep it there to protect it."

All the spiders talk like this. They either cannot follow the logic of a real conversation or they feel comfortable enough to give up their secrets to me.

A mosquito hits the web and she hurries off. I sigh. The rats have eaten what is left of the cheese and my stomach still growls. Soon I'll have to go into the forest to find more food. The banana trees won't be enough for all of us. I wonder how many bullets my father has left behind and shudder at the thought of having to kill anything, even one of the monkeys.

While the sun is setting, I go outside and wash my pants in a bucket. I have been naked most of the day and it feels both odd and liberating. It is something I'll get used to if, or when, my pants give out. I worry this will happen before I can find a way to the city for more clothes. And money. I'll need money for new pants but for that I need the hotel to be open. For the hotel to be open I need decent clothes. A naked boy as a bell hop will not be good for business. I am smaller than my father but I'll have to make his clothes work, I suppose. The thought of going back into his bedroom makes my breath catch in my throat.

*

When I return to the bird it is gone. Its body seems smaller, I think, because its soul has fled. I have no more tears. I'm becoming a river bed.

I strip off the sheet, wrap the bird carefully, and carry it outside. My clothes become stiff with drying sweat while I am digging its grave. I didn't think this all through when I began to tend to the birds, and there are humps of dirt all along the road that ends in front of the hotel. The guests will ask what they are and I can't very well say graves. I must remember to pat the earth flat, plant some shrubbery. This is the last of them though, my egret, my white-feathered bird. I think I've served them well.

*

The next day is taken up with unearthing a grave, not digging one. I begin excavating the dinosaur. I've stripped the ivy of its leaves and will use the stalks as rope to hold it together. It will have to do for a while. Now, if I can only decide how it's supposed to look.

I stand over the railing of the staircase, a pile of bones on the floor beneath me, green papaya tied with ivy in one hand. I toss it up, almost lose my balance as I lean over. It misses the beam and hits the floor, cracking open into two halves. I try again, this time tying the heavy brass bell on the front desk to the ivy. In three more tries I get it over and the first loop of makeshift rope dangles. I hoist up one bone, and then another. It's hard work and I have to secure the ivy to the railing as I adjust heights. When I'm done it doesn't look much like a dinosaur. It looks like a collection of dangling bones. At least the ribcage is decipherable.

Dinner conversation tonight consists of what to name the dinosaur. The lizards want the dinosaur to be named what they are named, but they didn't even have names until *I* named them so I am not going to consider their suggestions.

"Waterfall," a mouse squeaks hopefully.

"It needs to be scientific," I say. "Does anyone know Greek or Latin?"

The mouse's ears go back and she is clearly confused. I sigh.

"Green peas!" a spider shouts. "I have lost my egg sack!"

"Scientific," I say again. "Like amdrolopithicus or quentonandon."

"Quentonandon," the mouse suggests.

I sigh again and close my eyes.

There is a soft tapping at the glass of the open door. One of the moths is asking for permission to enter. "Only one," I tell them, and a large, brown moth flies in while the others walk like cards turned on their sides to the doorway.

It stands on bow-legs at the edge of the table. "Mammoth," it says. Its voice is like tissue ripping. I have never heard them speak.

"Why Mammoth?" I ask.

"Because it is one. We may not live long, but our memories are wood worms, hiding, hiding, buried, buried."

I rub my chin. The room has become quiet and everyone is waiting to hear what I will say.

"Mammoth!" I shout, standing up and knocking over my chair. I lean forward and slam my fists on the table; I hear my pants split. The moths are fluttering and my dinner guests are mumbling, but still, I can tell they're excited about our new addition. As a thanks for the suggestion, I leave a pillowcase on the balcony for the moths. They take to it immediately and are eager to help me name other things, like the hotel and the plant life, but I know the names for these already.

*

When my father died, he didn't look like my father at all. He looked like my grandfather, red and grey salted beard, sunken cheeks. The look of a man who used to be bigger. Too much skin the body no longer knows how to hold. He begged me to leave but I told him I wouldn't. I told him we'd been through too much for me to let him die alone. His was the first grave I ever dug, and the largest. I lined the bottom with orange and lemon rinds. I gritted my teeth and then cried every time I dropped him on the way from his bed to the front lawn. I thought for sure Saint Anthony would take care of me then, appear like some great general out of the mists to tell me what to do, how to live, but he didn't.

I am shocked when I go into my father's bedroom, not a large, opulent guest room, but a small servant's quarters room, and the imprint of his body, curled on its side, is still on the sheets. I do not remember it being there; I tell myself it has though, and turn my attention to the dresser, selecting taupe linen draw string pants. I have to pull the waist so tight that the legs bunch like bundled curtains. I decide it is very Robinson Crusoe and that it will be the new style.

As I stand, unwilling to go now that I've entered, the bedroom feels dark and smells stale. I have not been here since I took his body to burial and it's a forgotten shrine. There is a thin layer of dust on everything, all except for the sheets where my father's imprint is. I wonder if Saint Anthony has been sleeping in his memory.

*

I've pulled all the ivy off the hotel. I have scrubbed all the floors and washed the mirrors and windows with well water. The dust in the curtains has been batted out and plates and silverware are shining. The carpet is tacked to the stairs with finish nails I found, and tomorrow I will wash the sheets on the beds and air out the ones that are stored. I will polish the tarnish off the keys and then I will make sure Mammoth is clean and gleaming. When I am done, I will walk to the city, a three-day journey I think, and spread the word that the hotel is open again. The candelabras will fetch some money, they're silver through and through, and then I will buy food and hire a car back. I cannot wait to hear a human voice again.

Conversation at dinner is a somewhat unpleasant one. I have to tell the animals to clear out.

"Where are we supposed to go?" They ask in unison.

"You can stay," I tell them, "but not here, in this room. You can stay in my room."

They look at each other dubiously. They are not eager to share everything. But neither am I.

A beetle crawls out from under a placemat. "We were wild before," he says. "We can be wild again!" There is a surprising amount of enthusiasm in his voice. "Come on," he moans, and his iridescent back splits open into wings. "You've all gone soft. You wonder why the monkeys never come to dinner? It's because they don't want to ruin themselves. Every civilization falls, from Rome to Britain. Better never to go soft, if you ask me. Better to be wild than to find yourself unable to live without silk and hot water and food *given* to you."

My guests are stunned at this admonishment. They look to me to argue for them, but I can't.

"He's right, you know," I tell them. Two of the bats scoff and fly out the door, the beetles behind them. They are angry at me, or they know the truth of the words. I shrug my shoulders because I don't want to look hurt. "It's up to you," I say. "Maybe, maybe it would be better to not be cooped up in the room all the time." I regret the words the minute they leave my mouth. I don't want to be alone.

They begin to slink away and I know I will not see them again. You cannot tame the wild for its entire life. Only one mouse stays. Its ears are almost translucent and her veins pulse redder than normal, a kind of mouse blush. "I'll stay," she says. "Mirabell will stay."

"Mirabell is welcome to stay," I tell her, silently grateful that not everyone is abandoning the names I've so carefully crafted.

*

I must go into my father's room again for a shirt, not only to wear to town, but so that Mirabell can go with me. She is scared to stay here by herself when I leave. She cradles in the cuff of my pants, waiting for a chest pocket to slip into.

The sheets on the bed look different. The imprint on its side with its knees up towards the door is now facing the wall.

"Mirabell," I say, "have you ever seen the ghost my father said is here?"

"Of course," she says, as if this is commonplace.

"Why do you think I've never seen him?" I sit on the bed and run my hands over the folds of the cotton.

"I don't know," she admits. "He's around often enough."

"How often?"

"Well." She climbs up my pant leg and onto the bed where she can look up at me. "Not *every* night. Sometimes I sleep early. Sometimes

I'm just not where he is. But often. He sits with your birds when they are dying, strokes their chests and wings. Maybe he's confused now that there are no birds."

I do not tell her that the birds have not been here that long. That the ghost has had years to appear to me, and never has. She is just a mouse, and a hopeful one, and neither of us are privy to St. Andrew's desires.

In the dresser I pull out a white shirt with a large pocket. "This will have to do," I tell her. "Are you ready for the rounds?" She has never been a part of this ritual and is eager to see me climb the floors with the rifle. When it is uneventful and boring, she sighs against my ribs and says she wishes something exciting would happen.

In the lobby I check the front door; it is locked, like I left it, and Mammoth is creaking in its cradle of ivy. Tonight the fog is so thick and high that it settles just under the windows in my fourth story room. Mirabell is on the pillow next to me. I've never slept with a mouse before and worry I will roll over in my sleep and crush her. She assures me that my movement will wake her and she will move out of the way. I pray to Saint Andrew to help me, but Mirabell says he is not in the room.

*

When I wake it is full dark and I am shaking. I sit up and look at my hands, painted in shadows from the moon's light streaking through the window. But they are not shaking. The *shadows* are jumping, and the coverlet beneath my hands vibrates too. I am not shaking; the room is shaking. The window treatments are ocean waves and bits of plaster fall onto my face when I look to the ceiling above.

"Mirabell!" I cry, scrambling from the bed where I fall onto the floor, the ground roiling beneath me. I claw for the shirt I stripped off hours before and throw it on, eyes frantically searching the bed for her. She's huddled next to my pillow, her tail arced to curve around her hunched body. I scoop Mirabell up and drop her into the shirt pocket, rushing for the door as candle fixtures fall from the wall.

The stairs are groaning under us and the marble is splitting. Its sharp cracks are like gunfire and I think I may be screaming. Shadows leap at us while we flee down, down, and at the landing I see furniture beginning to slide on the floor, sliding away from us in the direction of the river bed.

Mirabell is wailing, an awful high-pitched noise that makes my ears buzz, and the ceiling to the left drops away, revealing dozens of dim stars.

At the base of the stairs I rush towards the front door and the whole hotel is shattering, shouting its death in the rumbling of the building as it disappears down the cliffside. The brass railings tear from the walls and I am running past the dining room towards the entry, but the dining room is already gone. The balcony is gone. In the moonlight I can see a few moths fluttering, confused at their disappearing beds.

In the lobby Mammoth is swinging from the vines. It looks to be dancing, and for a moment, I am convinced it has come to life. Its heavy body, moving for the first time in centuries, does not have enough room. The memory of what it was is too weighty and is breaking the hotel off into the river bed. One of the massive bones lurches and punches into the plaster, embeds there before the ground shifts again and rips the entire wall from the frame in the mammoth's desperate move for freedom.

There is no time to wonder, to question, and I pull the keys from behind the front desk. Miraculously they have not been knocked to the floor. I look at the tile buckling under my feet. And then I am fumbling with the key, the brass cold on my hand, and the front door is open and we are rushing through it.

I pitch forward, tripping on a pile of ivy in the dark, putting my hands out to catch myself, to protect Mirabell who is still crying in my pocket, her nose buried into one corner. I hear my left wrist snap, but there is no pain. Instead it is numb and when I roll over to look at it, it is a talon in the moonlight and the cliff around the hotel cracks. The whole building falls as if a bomb went off.

Then there is nothing. I lay on the ground looking at a space that should not be empty. I can hear muffled thumps and the sliding of rock into the gorge. At the edge of the cliff, trees are bending and swaying; somewhere behind us the monkeys are screeching in fright. And then it is over.

Gone. There is some dust, but quickly it is quiet again. The jungle hushes in the shock and confusion. We are all too scared to make any noise. My breathing is the loudest sound now. The hotel is gone. Like it was never there. The new ledge is raw dirt and old stone.

Mirabell's whiskers are scratching my chest and I lean forward, putting my good hand over my eyes.

We sit like this for a long time. Long enough for the monkeys to begin their howls again. Long enough for Saint Andrew to come find us.

He is short, much shorter than my father, and he wears a brown robe tied at the waist with rope. Through him I can see the banana trees, the clumps of dirt from dozens of graves. He motions for me to come join him.

"No, no," Mirabell quips. But she doesn't try to stop me. She stays right in my pocket as I stand, legs still quivering, my hand broken and bleeding, and follow him into the jungle.

DOOMSDAY NIGHT
LIVE

"You would not *believe* the day I've had." Satan is walking into his living room, brimstone hell-flames disappearing behind the closing door. His house is not what people typically think of for the King of the Underworld. It looks instead like an early-90s condo owned by retirees on the coast of Florida. It's decorated in pastel pinks and blushes; there are tacky lamps covered in seashells; and his coffee table is a large, ancient abalone covered with a sheet of glass. The flooring is mauve tile overlaid with reed mats. There are paintings from hotel shows—the kinds people used to see on commercials: *this Sunday only, all art must go!* Watercolors of a palm tree swaying in the wind, a beach home nestled in a sandy dune, two parrots huddling against each other in front of a waterfall.

His wife is knitting. She shakes her head at him, puts her needles down, and gets up to take his briefcase. His horns seem wilted, sagging.

"Is it hot in here?" he asks. "It feels hot."

"This is Hell sweetheart. Of course it's hot," his wife says.

Behind them, through a window framed with sand-colored curtains, a figure appears. He pauses as if to wave to the couple, but they don't notice him. He has a square-shaped mustache and a sun visor with an insignia for the Third Reich. His Hawaiian shirt is unbuttoned; his fanny pack is unzipped.

"Can you turn up the AC?" Satan asks.

*

Brigit is wondering when *Doomsday Night Live* began to go so downhill. She does not like this new Satan. She gets that he's supposed to look defeated, as worn out as everyone else because the apocalypse is taking so long, but he's so unlike Satan that he *can't* be Satan. It's only funny if it's satire.

Ten years ago, when the rapture started, some of the best comedians were left on earth. *Doomsday Night Live* was good then, but now the skits feel recycled, canned. Now it is hard to find good actors. Now it is hard to find anyone with any sense of humor.

The apocalypse will do that to you: bring you down, and lead to a life of mundanity. Most of the time Brigit wishes her mother had been willing to wait it out because it hasn't been as bad as people thought it would be, not sudden and overwhelming. Sudden and drawn out is more like it. Life continues on, even when the world is ending.

*

There were, of course, the expected things: pets turned on their masters, couples fought for no reason, saints rose from their graves. But there were no massive fires, no earth opening its hot maw to swallow people and buildings. Instead, it was getting colder. The sky was filling with grey clouds, and day and night it constantly rained soft ash despite nothing really burning. Plants suffocated without sun. People shoveled ash instead of snow. Brigit hadn't worn summer clothes in six years now and the winter jacket her mother left behind was becoming too small. *Big boned like your daddy*, her mother used to say when Brigit came home crying from grade school, her lunch box defaced with sharpie messages like FAT PIG and OINK OINK. Her mother had colored over them and then covered the black splotches with stickers and glue-gunned rhinestones.

This is what Brigit is looking at when she hears the soft tap on the back door—her old lunch box, which has fallen off the top of the freezer she's just opened to retrieve her dinner.

At first Brigit thinks she is imagining things. There's no need to be afraid anymore at night, because looters have grown bored. Also, now that the packs of wolves have died off and most of the really wicked people have killed each other, a night visit usually meant a neighbor needed to borrow something, or a neighbor was lonely, or a neighbor was coming to inform a loved one that they'd decided to move on. Brigit is alone though, and doesn't really have any people anymore.

She pulls the curtain aside and looks out. Darkness. Of course.

When she opens the door, standing in the yard, lit by the yellowed light filtering through the kitchen window, is a man.

"Hello," he says, putting his hands to his side. Then clasping them together. Then putting them to his sides again.

"Hello," Brigit says. She has never seen this man before. She is certain of it. Though she cannot see him clearly, she thinks he might be handsome—high cheekbones, a broad nose, long hair kept back in a ponytail. "Can I help you?"

"I'm hoping *you* can help *me*." As he steps closer, Brigit sees that he's dressed oddly. His shirt is big and boxy and as he climbs the steps of the porch, she can make out that it's comprised of some animal hide, struck through with twigs and dried leaves. "I know it's late notice, but you're expected, and you haven't at all responded to our letters or inquires or—"

"I'm sorry," Brigit says, backing up through the doorway, "but who are you?" She is beginning to worry now.

"I've forgotten all my manners," the man says, shaking his head and proffering a hand. "I am Saint Guthlac. We need to talk about your rapture."

*

As the end of days began, people started to disappear. The rapture, it was called, but Brigit didn't quite buy it. Not because she was raised atheist, but because it seemed like people were often taken indiscriminately. Her sixth-grade math teacher disappeared during lunch. When the students came back to class, her dress and pantyhose and shawl were on the floor but there was no Mrs. Bedford. She wasn't a nice person. She intentionally called on people she knew didn't understand the problem they were all working on and then made snooty noises when the poor student floundered at the whiteboard. She assigned homework that she graded but didn't correct. She gave pop quizzes on material they hadn't even covered. And *she* was taken. But Brigit's aunt was taken too—her mother's sister. Elise was a good woman who volunteered as a rape-crisis counselor. She wasn't a Christian, either. She'd been Muslim for over a decade.

There was debate at first: what this meant, the raptures of "wrong people." Scholars from Oxford and Cambridge and the Vatican sat around tables and broadcast their thoughts to the world. During one of these episodes of *The Theology Hour*, Brigit's mother was on the sofa and said simply, "All these people saying all this stupid shit. Like we're ever going to know what's really going on."

That was about three years in, when Brigit was twelve. And even being young, Brigit knew her mother had a point. No one *saw* people disappear. They just did—poof. One minute a wife would be talking to her husband in the kitchen and he'd turn around to open a drawer and then she'd just be gone, a pile of clothes left on the linoleum.

"I don't want to be taken," her mother had said, changing the station. This, of course, was back when there were still multiple stations, when people *could* change the channel. "Who knows where they go. And if you ask me, the fact they go there naked…that's creepy. What kind of god strips you down anyway?"

Brigit had wanted to say, *Maybe that's the point. Maybe if there's a heaven and you get there you have to be stripped of everything—bare your soul,* but her mother seemed so adamant. Her mother who always changed the channel when the theological debates came on. The mother who said she didn't want to go through chemo. The mother who never really seemed to believe in anything other than her daughter being perfect the way she was.

*

Brigit used to have dreams about the people who were raptured. In one dream she was with a raptured woman, but she was in the woman's handbag, the kind made for carrying small dogs, and she and the woman ended up at a convention center where everyone was dressed for a luau. In another she was with a tribe of Native Americans who were being chased by white men with guns along a river and when they jumped off a waterfall, rather than be shot, they were teleported to a baseball diamond where Miller Lite was sponsoring a taste test. All the cans of beer got raptured and the spectators in the stands got angry.

These dreams were never scary, just wacky and weird and when Brigit woke up from them her mouth was always sore like she'd been smiling too hard for too long.

Freshman year's creative writing class asked them to write a short story about rapture. Most people wrote about bright lights and golden gates and sensations like flying and falling at once, but Brigit wrote about one of her dreams: the one where she was a manager of a candy store and all the workers were excited because they were getting a shipment of a new gummy candy—gummy centipedes—but the man who was supposed to bring the shipment was raptured in the parking lot so no one brought the box in and the candy melted all ooey gooey together in a hot van and no one got to see what they looked like.

Of course, Brigit changed the story a bit from her dream. In her dream she was helping the man bring the boxes in and then he was naked and telling her he didn't want to go as he started to float up and up, Brigit grabbing the box he was still holding onto and trying to pull him down. But she was pulled up instead, and she hung from the box as they both ascended and she kept looking up to keep from looking down but that left her staring at his shriveled penis and testicles and he kept apologizing about the sight. And then they were on the moon and the gummy centipedes had come alive and were doing a conga line.

In class, she was forced to read her work aloud as some of the mean girls snickered and Brenda—who was raptured a week later—could be heard saying, *Of course there would be candy*—and Stephanie, who was not raptured, responded, *It's not even hot enough to melt things in cars anymore.* Their teacher didn't shut the girls up because clearly he'd already stopped caring, and about a month after they all finished the year, the teacher shot himself with a .22 inside the Presbyterian Church.

But that day at lunch, after she'd read her story, the captain of the girl's track team, Melena, sat with Brigit and told her that she liked it. *It's like Doomsday Night Live*, Melena said. *Like it's funny and serious at the same time and not what you expect but it still sort of makes sense. I bet you could be a writer for them.* And then, when Melena saw Stephanie eyeing them, said, *My girlfriend isn't very funny.*

Brigit had thought about that briefly: maybe becoming a writer. She wrote a few dreams into skits and didn't think they were half-bad.

For a few weeks she'd let herself believe she could do it—she'd never go to college now, not that they'd stay open even if she could—but with the internet down and gone for good she couldn't google the TV show, find out who she might email, even get an address where she might send in one of her skits as a kind of résumé.

The one good thing that had come out of the short story incident was that Melena started paying attention to Brigit. She never asked Brigit out, but she did stop Brigit in the hallways to ask how her mother was doing, and sometimes, they'd eat lunch together. Once, Melena even brought over a Tupperware container full of raspberry scones. Brigit had wondered where the fruit came from.

*

"What are you wearing?" Brigit asks the man. She's thought of a lot of questions in the few seconds that have passed but this is the one that comes out.

"This?" he asks, looking down at himself. "Oh, it's a hair shirt."

"What's a hair shirt?"

"It's…uncomfortable. That's what it is," the man says, shrugging his shoulders and wincing. "Are you going to ask me in?"

"Are you like, a vampire? Do I have to invite you?"

"Vampires don't exist," the man responds as if Brigit should know this. "It's just polite not to enter a house unless expressly invited to."

"Then come on, I guess."

Inside, an awful *Doomsday Night Live* skit is ending. A bunch of angels have descended from Heaven to parlay with Satan's minions and they are all sitting down to eat at the most awkward dinner party in history. The angels' mouths are too delicate for the ghost-pepper enchiladas and the demons are apologizing profusely; they keep offering other dishes, but their tongues are immune to spicy heat and they don't understand that each is worse than the last. The angels begin to have indigestion. They are farting and it sounds like trumpets.

"Oh, Lord," the saint says, looking at the TV. "How embarrassing."

The local rapture banner is beginning to scroll across the bottom of the screen. 10:30 every night, on the dot. Brigit sees names she doesn't recognize, people from the area who have disappeared.

She is more annoyed by the Saint than she wants to admit. When they first started appearing, people thought they were zombies. They climbed out of graves and tombs, bits of relics flew from churches and bodies re-assembled in town squares. There was a panic until the saints didn't do anything at all. They walked into forests or deserts and just disappeared. Now there is one in her living room, keeping her from getting in bed. She is supposed to go to work tomorrow.

"Sorry to barge in like this," the man apologizes, "but we're running out of time."

"Running out of time for what?" Brigit sits on the sofa, muting the TV. The angels think the demons are making fun of them and have decided to leave the party, negotiations incomplete.

"The end of the world."

"You mean this isn't going to go on forever?" At this point, Brigit really expected it to, each year dragging on—people have gotten used to the idea that they'll just die out like the dinosaurs—an upcoming ice age.

"Oh, no, of course not. Sooner or later God's going to wake up and see what's happened and be mortified. Get it?" The man laughs. "Mortified? Death? Never mind. You're last on my list and the sooner you make up your mind the sooner I can crawl back into my fens and get some much-needed rest. The end days are really taxing."

"Make up my mind? About what?"

"About the rapture. I've been trying to contact you, but your mind is all over the place. I can't tell what you want. Some dreams say yes. Some say no. If you want to go, you need to just say so and come with me."

"Look," Brigit says, "you may be a saint or whatever, but I don't *have* to do anything." She's thinking about the stranger danger seminar from fifth grade. How a grown-up woman came to speak to them about how she was kidnapped as a child and was held hostage for six years. Afterwards all the kids were fingerprinted, and their pictures were taken. When she'd come home with a packet for her mother to complete—blood type, dentist's name, etc.—her mother had said that was the last thing they needed to worry about. She'd said the school was being absurd, causing panic for no reason.

"Okay, look, I shouldn't really be telling you this, but whatever. I don't think it's going to matter. You know how in the bible, God rested on the seventh day? Here's the deal. He's still resting. People think that God is on their time, but he's not. He's God. He's got his own time, and it doesn't work like yours. A day for you may be a millennium for him. A day for you might be a day for him too, but who knows how time really works anyway. In a few days he's going to wake up and realize everything's gone to Hell in a handbasket and he's just going to start over again. So you can come with me or stay here and get wiped out. It's up to you."

"But go *where?*"

"...to heaven."

"There really is a heaven? Is my mom there?"

"I don't know."

"You don't know who all is in heaven?" Brigit asks.

"Not like I've got a scroll I can check against."

"This is not what I thought it was going to be."

"It's not what most people thought it was going to be. I thought there would be winged devils. But nope. Nada. Not a single devil, wings or no wings," the saint says while shrugging.

"If you don't have a scroll about who should be in heaven, what kind of list do you have that says I need to go?"

"Uh…" One of the saint's hands reaches into his hair-shirt and pulls out a napkin. He squints at it.

Brigit can see through the thin paper and says, "Give me that." She reaches between them and plucks the thing right out of his hands. "Ronald McDonald. Beavis and Butthead. Brigit Mackle. Are you fucking kidding me?"

The phone rings and Brigit gets up, crumpling the napkin in her hand. "Hello?"

There's laughing on the other end and the telltale snort-choke of Susan Levis, Stephanie's second in command. "This, is, uh, God," a badly disguised voice says. "I'm just wondering…"

"You all are some really nasty bitches," Brigit says. "You know the world is ending. There are more important things right now. More important than pretending like popularity matters. You think because you get to finish high school that you're better than me? Grow the fuck up." She slams down the receiver.

In the living room she tells the pretender to get out.

"I'm really sorry, miss," the man says. "But they had canned pineapple. *Pineapple.* When was the last time you had pineapple?"

"It's the end of the fucking world and you came in here pretending to be a saint for a can of pineapple? This is fucked up. This whole thing is fucked up." Brigit throws the napkin at him, which trails daintily to the floor. "Get out or I'll call the cops."

*

Brigit dreams in *Doomsday Night Live*. Satan and his wife are away on campaign and two little devils are housesitting. Mrs. Satan has left clear instructions, drawn in blood, on a sheet of parchment attached to the fridge with a magnet that looks like a shellacked hermit crab. It should be easy: 1) feed Cerberus four hundred cups of food once in the morning and once at night, 2) answer the phone but take down any messages including names and numbers, and 3) don't under any circumstance go down into the basement.

The two red-painted, wizened half-men are stupid. They spill their tom kha soup on the list and the blood smears. They cannot remember what they should and shouldn't do. Then they are playing baseball in the living room and when devil number two doesn't make his catch, the ball spins full force into a vase on the mantel. It shatters. The devils try to piece the vase back together but none of the glue will hold because it's so hot in hell. The vase keeps falling apart and finally it's so covered in tacky mess that they give up, and when Satan and Mrs. Satan return and notice the vase missing, Satan looks right at the camera and laughs, *You guys*, while the devils slink away out the door.

*

The country's new motto is *Save, Conserve, and Survive*. Even if Satan never emerges from the depths of Hell—wherever that is—arable land is disappearing and power grids are draining.

Conserve is a synonym for reuse, which is how Brigit got her job. She made that statement to the manager of the co-op which has kept her supplied. Luckily, (or unluckily for his family), the man at the top of the regional credit union, before he suffocated himself in his garage with exhaust fumes, wiped clean every record of every mortgage his clients had to pay. Brigit suspected it was only a matter of time until some bank tracked down something and her house went up for grabs. But maybe not. No one was buying houses anymore. There weren't enough people to fill them all. The co-op paid enough for her to live, sans car, sans mortgage. Food and power were the only things she needed.

Brigit's job is in clothing. She sorts through incoming clothes delivered in giant, twine-wrapped piles by a man with shaggy red hair who drives a repurposed U-Haul van. She must first determine what is in good enough condition to be "sold" with clothing coupons, and then she divides them into smaller piles based on gender and age and size. Then she lugs them across the warehouse to the laundresses who wash them. She does this Tuesday through Saturday, often arriving home that last day just in time to catch *Doomsday Night Live*. She's put in a job request transfer form explaining that the clothing aggravates her allergies. This is a lie. She cannot stand working in the clothing section of the co-op because it reminds her of the lives everyone has been robbed of.

Some days she comes home almost crying because of the smells. People have smells, even if there is no longer widespread use of perfume or cologne or scented soap. Sometimes the clothes smell like someone was wearing the sweater or flannel while cooking a delicious meal: cinnamon or something green, oregano perhaps. Sometimes they smell like smoke. Brigit knows this is more likely due to a house fire, but the smell elicits memories of Girl Scout campouts and the onset of fall, a season that no longer exists. Other times they smell simply like body odor—gym class. And sometimes they smell like lemon pledge— the same lemon pledge her mother used to clean the sideboard in the dining room.

Sometimes Brigit steals clothing that smells like something she likes: mothballs and her aunt's linen closet where she played hide and seek; lavender, the herb that grew in her back yard; Paloma Picasso, the perfume her mother wore, that she lamented when she could no longer find it—some woman having hoarded it for years, used it sparingly for special events, left like teasing ghosts on clothing for Brigit to rub her face on.

*

While walking home, Brigit looks for Tanny Dupree who delivers the "mail". Tanny hasn't quite gotten the hang of the apocalypse. Or maybe she has. Maybe that's why every week Tanny makes her rounds, re-delivering old mail that no one cares about. Junk mail. Old advertisements for roofing companies, pizza coupons, Val-Paks stuffed with offers from dentist offices or house washing and discount haircut coupons. Tanny delivers the mail on Tuesdays. On Friday nights she sneaks around and removes from mailboxes what hasn't been taken, and then, the following Tuesday, she redistributes it all.

Brigit finds Tanny on Westchester. "Hey," she says, pulling the vest she's gotten from work out of her bag. "I thought you might like this."

"You thought right." Tanny sets her satchel down and slips on the puffy vest. It's navy blue, the only color she wears on Tuesdays on account of her "federally mandated job". She snaps the front closed and looks down at herself. "You know," she begins, "it would be really nice if we could get some uniforms."

"Well, until then."

"Yeah, until then."

Brigit turns to leave and Tanny stops her. "You want your mail?"

"Sure."

Tanny searches through her satchel and hands Brigit a wad of envelopes and crinkled, loose papers. "There's a letter, too. Guy didn't have postage, but I won't tell if you don't tell."

Indeed, there is a yellow envelope on top with her address—no name—and when she turns it over, Brigit sees the envelope has been resealed with new tape.

"I hope it's jury duty," Brigit says, and both women laugh.

Inside is a note scrawled on yellow legal pad paper, and Saint Guthlac, i.e. Sven, is apologizing again. He's offered to make it up to her, show her a *real* saint, if she's willing to meet him on Friday in front of the old pizza parlor.

"Anything good?" Tanny asks, trying to read the message upside down.

"No. You should have made him pay."

"I don't know," Tanny muses. "He looked pretty down in the dumps already."

*

Brigit has only dreamed of her mother once since she died. In the dream, her mother was still alive and worked in a petting zoo. She was preparing the animals for their rapture.

"Mom," Brigit said, "this is absurd."

Her mother was telling the baby sheep about how they had been there—not them specifically, but their ancestors—at the birth of Jesus Christ.

"This isn't even you," Brigit complained. "You don't believe in God."

Her mother put her hands over one of the lamb's ears. "Hush, they'll hear you."

"Mom, they don't understand words."

"Maybe you just don't understand sheep," one bleated out.

"Mom, come on. We have to go."

"Go where? Where is there to go?" Her mother looked around and

Brigit looked too. They were in a high-ceilinged barn and the slats of wood were far enough apart that Brigit could see the stars and the moon. It had been a long, long time since she'd seen them.

"Sit down," her mother said, "and wait with me."

"Wait for what? Mom, this isn't right."

"Everything is right. Everything is exactly as it should be. Let's just wait together, you and I and the sheep."

But Brigit didn't want to wait for the rapture of the sheep. If people lost their clothes then perhaps the sheep lost their wool, or worse, their skin, and suddenly, Brigit was frightened of what she might see.

"I do wonder," her mother said, "where they go. It doesn't make any sense, you know."

Brigit knew it didn't make any sense. She remembered how the woman who stocked the soft drinks at the gas station was raptured. How afterward the guy at the counter said she was lucky because she'd been stealing shit for months and the manager was about to come down on her.

"Did I ever tell you about my sister?" Brigit's mother asked.

"Tell me what?"

"Did I ever tell you about what she did in high school? The senior class prank?"

"Mom we really don't have time for this." The sheep were beginning to glow.

"That poor sheep. That poor girl."

"Mom!"

The sheep were beginning to float. They did not become undone. They made loud noises as their legs dangled awkwardly.

"You never really know people, do you," her mother asked, letting go of the sheep struggling in her lap. "Do you know what I always thought was funny? All these people debating the end of times. All these people thinking the rapture is some great thing, being taken up into heaven. You know, centuries ago people thought the end of days would result in heaven on earth. If that's true, where is everyone going?"

"I don't know, mom."

Brigit's mother was beginning to glow too. The cloth of her dress was unfolding. "Satan is a tricky bugger," she said, and then shot herself in the head.

*

Brigit is shopping at the Stop & Shop, counting her food vouchers at the counter when in walks Melena. She shakes the ash from her coat like it's snow and heads straight to the coolers in the back.

Brigit tries to shove the cans the cashier had just rang up into her bag as quickly as she can, but Melena is only here for one thing, a gallon of milk, which she brings up to the counter before Brigit can make her escape.

"Hey," Melena says. "Haven't seen you around for a while."

The cashier makes a note in his log for Melena's purchase. People like Melena didn't need to count out food vouchers. No one was worried they didn't have enough money. Melena's dad made a killing when the end of the world started and he owned the only gun store in a thirty-mile radius.

"Been working since mom died." Brigit turns to leave, but Melena sticks beside her.

"Yeah, I was sad to hear about that. Did you have a funeral?"

Brigit shakes her head. "Nope. But you've missed some really awesome parties. You know, teenager at home, alone, no parents."

Brigit watches Melena fight for words then adds, "That was a joke," wondering if there *were* in fact parties that went on and if Melena had been thinking of an excuse for why she hadn't shown up for Brigit's imagined ones.

"Yeah, right."

They stand outside the Stop & Shop, Brigit angled to head east, Melena's bike facing north. Melena puts her milk in the crate bungee-corded behind her seat.

"I really wish you were still in school," Melena admits finally, not looking at Brigit, but past her, across the street at the shuttered pie diner. "It's gotten...awful."

"Really?"

"Yeah. We don't even have a track team anymore, you know. Or we do, but there's no way to compete against other schools. Too many variables, coach says."

"Honestly, I'm amazed it's gone on as long as it has. School, I mean, not track."

Melena nods. "And now that Stephanie's gone..."

"Gone?" Brigit's hands clench and relax. *Of course* Stephanie got taken. Of course.

"Sometimes I just feel really alone," Melena adds. "Like we're all waiting in this terrible loop that keeps replaying and we're waiting for it to be over and every day just starts the same thing up all over again. I'm thinking of quitting school. Change of pace."

"You could come work at the co-op," Brigit laughs.

"Maybe." Melena seems to take the suggestion seriously. "At the least I need to *do* something. Somehow calculus just doesn't seem fulfilling right now."

"Was it ever?" Brigit's shoulder is starting to burn and she realizes how tense she is. She switches the strap to the other shoulder. Tries to relax her body.

"Not really. I'm actually thinking about going out and chopping down some trees."

"Lumberjack?"

"At some point we're going to need firewood. Might as well get started, you know."

"You should come by sometime. Maybe. If you want to talk," Brigit blurts out. "My mom's gone, Traci's gone, Maureen's gone. I mean my friends are gone, too."

"That could be fun," Melena says, straddling her bike.

*

On Thursday, when Brigit gets home, there is a notice on her door. She has exceeded her power allowance, and her electric will not be restored until Monday, when everyone's allowance resets.

She thinks of all the times she's fallen asleep with the TV on, heating a house big enough for a family of four when her allowance is only for one. She's left too many lights on, drawn the curtains shut against the lamp lights on the street, all because she doesn't want to be seen alone, inside.

That night, Brigit huddles under blankets with her mittens on, pretending she is a train-hopper, a homeless woman living off the land. She knows she's too old for games like this, but fantasy is often better than reality—especially when the world is ending but no one knows how long it will take.

When she tires of this, Brigit puts on ski pants over her flannel pajama bottoms, a sweater over her thermal, and then a coat over the sweater. She wraps a scarf around her neck, and dons the beanie she got from the co-op, a pink one with little crocheted pig ears atop the head.

Brigit walks the streets. She looks in people's windows. She feels like Tiny Tim, or was it Oliver Twist, desperate to find an inside, a place to belong. Maybe it was the Little Matchstick Girl.

She marvels at Tanny's flowerpots full of plastic irises, the terra cotta decoupaged with pages of old magazines, placed perfectly in the glow of her porch lights. She crosses the street and picks up her pace, acts like she has some where to be, when a man she does not know comes out of his home to shovel his ash, to replace the decorative garden flag—turkey to Christmas tree—and to stare at nothing, just standing with his head raised and arms wide, thinking he is alone and unseen.

Brigit stops a few blocks over, trying to remember who she's seeing. The elderly couple that owned the bookstore—Ruth and George? They are sitting on their sofa, their bodies in profile, and Brigit thinks they may be playing a card game. Ruth is laughing, and then George is laughing too. Ruth picks up a glass, takes a sip, and George says something that makes her sputter it all out. She is smiling wide and patting her wet blouse.

Brigit is about to turn around and go home, the ash dissolving in her eyes and giving her what will become a migraine, when she sees the telltale red banner across the screen on the TV in the corner of the old folk's living room.

Brigit creeps across their lawn. She stands outside the window, knowing she can see in but that they cannot see out. She thanks an unknown God that Ruth and George are hard of hearing, that there are still such things as closed captioning, even during the apocalypse.

The TV report scrolls across the screen: Simeon Stylites had appeared. When the sun rose over Aleppo that morning the saint could be seen standing on a tall pillar. Crowds gathered and one American who'd been stuck there since the planes were grounded said the saint had finally floated down, refusing food and water, going so far as to slap a woman's hand when she forcefully proffered a cup to him. He said the saint didn't seem very nice.

Brigit doesn't know what makes her more uneasy: that the saints are reappearing or that this saint isn't wandering off into the desert. Brigit remembers a movie she watched with her mother once. It was about a boy who was a transient and carried his lunch tied in a red bandana attached to a stick he rested on one shoulder. Brigit had been enamored with the boy: with the idea that he did just fine without parents or school—he was better, in fact, because of it.

*

There is a lice outbreak at the co-op. No one can find the source of the buggers, but people are coming in and complaining. Joshua says the sofa he picked up last week is suspect. Mrs. Rand says all four of her children were sent home from school. Patrick Kirk actually spreads his hair apart and shows Brigit the little white things. She almost vomits.

"Well, I don't know what they want us to do," Brigit's boss says, standing just inside the front doors and surveying the business. "Look at all this. How would we be able to clean it all?"

The co-op has collected items from everyone in town: dishes, pillows, toys, clothes, furniture, artwork, bedding, lawn care items, pet accessories.

Brigit's boss sighs. "You know," she begins, her eyes roving over the room, "when the apocalypse started, I never thought about lice. I thought about that movie—the joke one where all the celebrities are weathering the end of the world. I thought about making sure I had enough Snickers bars." She laughs. "Fucking Snickers bars. I was thinking prison money. Now look at us, a whole town infected with lice. Lice is the problem. Not food. Not… whatever else we worried about that hasn't happened. Lice."

Brigit doesn't know what to say back. She actually finds it funny, in a dark way, that lice have found a home here. She wonders if they'll keep living after all the humans are gone.

"Welp," her boss says. "What do you think?"

"I think we're going to have to learn to live with itchy heads."

*

Melena is waiting outside when Brigit gets off work. "I came to tell you," she says, "that it's the end of the world."

Brigit looks at her questioningly.

"Sorry. Bad joke."

The two girls walk side by side, past the old Thai restaurant, past the old paint your own pottery store, past the old cat café.

"I tried to call you," Melena says, "but your phone was disconnected."

"Yeah, my power's off."

"I didn't go to school today. I think I'm done with it."

Brigit looks at Melena, the dark hair curling out from under her cap, lips flaking and chapped. "And? What are you going to do instead?"

"I think I need to wait to see if my parents make me go back. Right now, I'm just going to enjoy the break."

"Did you hear about Saint Simeon?"

The girls cut through the parking lot of a shuttered gas station, the shelves inside the small store standing, but empty.

"Sure did," Melena replies. "My mom spent all night crossing herself and praying in Spanish."

"You believe in saints?"

"What kind of question is that?" Melena kicks the ash on the ground in front of her. "I mean, yeah, I do. How can I not? Don't you believe?"

Brigit wants to tell Melena about Guthlac, fake Guthlac, Sven. She wants to launch into a long meditation on the nature of saints, and the apocalypse, and loneliness. She wants to explain how it's possible for one to both believe and not believe, but she's afraid to bore Melena. To scare her away with philosophy meanderings. So instead she tells Melena that there may be a saint in town, and asks if she wants to see it.

"Is this a joke?" Melena asks.

"Nope. Heard from a little birdie that there's a flesh and blood saint."

"That's very Saint Francis of you."

The girls laugh.

"Yeah, I'll go," Melena says. "What could it hurt?"

*

The old pizza parlor is kind of a fascinating place. At least, it feels that way to Brigit. Once a month the business starts up at 3pm. The owners—the Kalbeks—turn the lights on. Bring wagons full of cooperatively collected food. By 6pm, Mangia Man is open for business to all who have contributed something. Takie Kalbek stands at the door with a list and checks names against it. People who haven't contributed can stand in the wait line to see if there's anything left.

Brigit used to eat at Mangia Man with her mother before the apocalypse started. There was an arcade—a dark room full of glowing, neon tubes—with machines that spit out tickets for winners. At the prize desk, children could turn them in for footlong laffy taffy, yo-yo's, ring pops, sparkly crayons. Every time they ate at Mangia Man, Brigit's mother would give her three dollars in quarters and let her run off to the other side of the restaurant. Only now that Brigit cups her hands against Mangia Man's windows, looking at the red pleather booths, the terrible hotel carpet, the 70s-style chandeliers, does she wonder what her mother spent that time doing. When Brigit was smashing buttons and making race car noises, her mother must have been sitting alone at their table, drinking soda or wondering if she should eat Brigit's pizza crusts.

"I'm sorry I was so young," Brigit whispers, stepping back and looking up at the business's sign to see an abandoned bird's nest inside the hollow of Mangia's G.

"And I'm sorry I was a dick."

Brigit spins to see Sven. He's dressed in a long green trench coat and gloves with the tips of the fingers cut off.

"You ready?" he asks.

"We gotta wait for my friend."

Sven steps back. "Oh, I don't know about that. I didn't tell the saint anyone else was coming."

Brigit frowns. "Are you for real?"

"Pinch me."

"Aren't I supposed to pinch myself?"

"Do that then."

Brigit sees Melena behind Sven, approaching from across the street. Brigit can see Melena's lipstick, bright orange. "That's her now," Brigit says.

Sven turns to look at Melena and then steps to the side as she approaches them. Melena looks between them, uncertain.

"Melena, this is Sven," Brigit says. "He's gonna take us to the saint."

"Don't I know you?" Melena asks. Now that she is right beside Brigit, the scent of baby powder is in the air.

"Unless you live under a bridge, I doubt it. Do you live under a bridge?"

"No."

"Then it's nice to meet you." Sven waves for the girls as he begins walking off.

"You sure about this?" Melena asks.

Brigit shrugs. "What could happen that's worse than the end of the world?"

*

Brigit and Melena follow Sven into the Oakwood sub-division and past ranch style houses made of light-colored brick. They follow him into Oakwood park with its broken swings and rusty see-saw, the merry-go-round that's come unhinged, the park benches covered in ash. They follow him into the greenbelt and see markers for the discgolf course no one uses anymore, metal workout stations with signs illustrating how to do proper pull-ups and crunches. They see an old red cooler, open and empty. A jacket on the ground. Crushed cigarette boxes.

As they walk deeper into the trees, their feet sinking into ash, into dead foliage, into the soft earth beneath, Melena reaches for Brigit's hand, and Brigit gives it.

"Alright." Sven stops in front of them and holds up his hand. "You got to be quiet now."

Brigit and Melena come up behind him, trying to see around his tall body.

There is a clearing in the trees, and in that clearing is a hovel. That is the best word Brigit thinks she has to explain the structure, a squat little thing about as big as her bathroom with a roof of browned pine branches.

Sven puts a finger to his lips.

They stand there like that for a long time, the three of them. Melena's hand is sweaty and when Brigit's fingers twitch, they glide over the wetness. Eventually, the three begin to hear singing.

There is no door to the hovel, but there is a purple and gold striped comforter nailed up over an opening. This is pulled to the side, and a small woman emerges.

She is dressed in a pantsuit, work boots, and green scarf. She is holding a coffee cup in her hands. She looks around, stops her singing, and says, "I know you're there."

"Damnit." Sven's shoulder's droop.

"What in the world?" Melena whispers.

"You might as well come out," the woman calls. She retreats back into her hovel and then comes out again, folded lawn chairs in her arms. She's struggling to lug them all out.

Sven moves forward and helps her, taking two and opening them up.

Brigit and Melena are still holding hands, still hiding in the trees.

"I don't think that's a saint," Melena says, craning her neck to get a better look.

"I don't think you would know a holy person if one bit you on the butt," the woman calls.

Brigit can't help but chuckle. "Come on."

There are four folding chairs, and the saint and Sven are sitting in two of them. Brigit removes her hand from Melena's and takes the third. Melena stays standing. "Which saint are you?" she asks.

"I don't know what makes you think I'm a saint," the woman says, making side eyes at Sven. "One does not have to be a saint to be a messenger for the gods."

Melena looks distrustful, the right side of her mouth frowned down, but she takes the fourth chair, and now all of them are circled together in the middle of the woods as the sun is setting, bringing with it the cold so many try to escape this time of day.

"What do we do now?" Brigit finally asks when no one talks or moves, while Sven and Melena seem content to sit and do and say nothing.

"What would you like to do?" the holy woman asks.

"Well…" Brigit trails off.

"Maybe I'll tell you a story," the holy woman begins. "About the end of the world. Not *the* world, of course. *The* world never ends, it just changes."

"Oh lord," Sven says. "Here we go again."

"What I have learned, over all these years, these decades, these centuries," the holy woman says, ignoring Sven's commentary, "is that any story can be told and turned into something different than it is. Listeners, or readers, will fill in the gaps. People like to make their own meaning, to feel they are a part of creation through their own insertions. Listen to me girls, because *this* man has no use for stories."

"It's true," Sven says. "I am so tired of stories."

"I will tell you a story about the end of the world," the holy woman says.

"But I don't want it to be the end of the world," Melena protests, shifting in her chair.

"Oh, hush now, it's okay." The holy woman is out of her chair and crouching in front of Melena. The woman is small but large, and Brigit's vision seems to expand, or collapse. All she can see is the cotton twill of a navy blue blazer. No sky. No trees. No ash.

"I am going to tell you a story," Brigit hears the holy woman say, "and as I tell the story, it will start to sound familiar. And as it starts to sound familiar, you will recognize that it is the end."

ACKNOWLEDGEMENTS

"An Oracle" first appeared in *Bourbon Penn*, issue 10

"Amarna" first appeared in *Crack the Spine*, issue 132

GWENDOLYN PARADICE is hearing impaired, queer, and a member of the Cherokee Nation. Her writing has earned nominations for both the Pushcart and Best American Essays, and her nonfiction, fiction, and poetry have appeared in *Assay*, *Crab Orchard Review*, *Brevity*, *Fourth River*, *Booth*, and others. She retains a MA in Nonfiction from the University of North Texas, an MFA from Bennington College, and is currently pursuing a PhD at the University of Missouri, where she lives with her partner. When she's not weightlifting, playing video games, or trying to read all the books she's amassed, she writes speculative fiction, nontraditional nonfiction, and bends genre.